ROSE OF SKIBBEREEN

BOOK 3

By John McDonnell

Copyright © 2013 John McDonnell

All rights reserved

ISBN-13: 9798645676186

Discover other titles at John McDonnell's Amazon page: amazon.com/author/johnmcdonnell.

FOREWORD TO BOOK 3

This is the third book in the "Rose Of Skibbereen" series. The series is a fictional story about Rose Sullivan, a girl from Skibbereen, in County Cork, who sails to America in 1880 to find work as a domestic servant, so that she can send money back to her impoverished family in Ireland. At her going away party in Ireland she meets a young man named Sean McCarthy, a handsome fellow with a beautiful singing voice. In America she runs into him again, but now he is calling himself Peter Morley.

What Rose doesn't know is that Peter killed a British soldier in anger back in Ireland, and he is running from his crime. Rose conceives a child with Peter, and she is forced to leave her job as a servant for the Lancasters, a wealthy family in Philadelphia. Peter and Rose marry and have three sons, but Peter leaves Rose and the children on New Year's Day of 1900, because he has fallen in love with a young English woman named Edith Jones who is visiting Philadelphia. He marries Edith without telling her of his previous marriage to Rose. In fact, he makes up a new name for himself: James Francis.

Rose struggles to keep her family afloat, and at times she is visited by the spirit of her dead mother, who talks to her of the unseen world of fairies and spirits. Rose's oldest son Tim becomes a hopeless alcoholic and her youngest son Willy is killed in an accident, leaving Rose with only one remaining son, Paul.

Rose has had a hard life as a single mother, but she gets help from an unlikely source: Martin Lancaster, a member of the family for whom she worked as a domestic servant years before. Martin has fallen in love with Rose, and he seeks her out after her husband leaves her. He takes care of her and she gradually falls in love with him.

When Book Three starts Rose is 73, married to Martin Lancaster, and she is worried that things are not going well between her son Paul and his wife Lucy. She is troubled by more contact with the spirit world. The Great Depression is in full swing, and there are rumblings of war in Europe.

To find Books 1 and 2 of "Rose Of Skibbereen" go to: amazon.com/author/johnmcdonnell.

CHAPTER ONE

November 2, 1935

"Why, I can hardly believe my own eyes. Is it Rose Sullivan I'm looking at?"

Rose stared back at the well-dressed woman who was standing at her counter in the Wanamaker's Ladies' Dress Department. The woman had on a fox trimmed gray coat, there was a string of pearls at her neck, and her silver hair peeked out from under a black wide-brimmed hat tilted at a jaunty angle. She had a round, fleshy face and merry green eyes, and although she looked familiar, Rose could not place her as someone she knew.

"You don't recall me? Why, I suppose that's to be expected. It's been near 50 years since we last spoke. It's me, Mary Driscoll herself. Do you not remember that name, Rose?"

It was like an electric shock to Rose. "Is it you, Mary?" she said. "This is a surprise, after so many years. To be sure, I am sorry I did not recognize you."

"Well, I doubt you've been thinking much of poor old Mary Driscoll all these years," Mary said. "I admit I look different, though. I've come up in the world, as you can see." She adjusted her fur and struck a pose.

"Aye, you always wanted fine things, as I remember," Rose said. "I'm glad it has all worked out for you."

"And what of you, Rose?" Mary said. "How are things with you?"

Rose saw that Mary was looking at her plain gray dress, the parsimonious touch of makeup on her face, her white hair cut in a sensible bob.

"Fine, to be sure," Rose said. "I am surviving, Mary. Now, can I help you? I take it you are here to buy a dress."

"Oh, Rose, don't be so formal," Mary said, taking her hand. "We grew up together in Skibbereen, remember? I know there was a falling out between us, but it's late in life and we should forget those old grievances. Let's not hold on to those grudges the way so many of our countrymen like to do."

"I am holding no grudge," Rose said, taking her hand back. "It is only that this is my place of employment, Mary. I cannot be standing around chatting with the clientele about times past, you see. I am lucky enough to have a job in these hard years, and I want to keep it."

"I understand, Rose," Mary said. "But I believe it's a good sign that I happened upon you today. I hardly ever come to Wanamaker's on my own, you understand. I usually send my maid Christine to pick up a few things for me. I'm only here because I'm leaving for Ireland tomorrow and I needed to buy a few last minute items, and Christine is busy with other errands."

Rose detected a gleam in Mary's eyes at the mention of a servant. Of course, Mary would want her to know that she was able to afford her own servants now, that the wheel had turned since those days so long ago when she was a servant for others.

"Anyway," Mary said. "'Tis a miracle, me running into you like this, and I don't want to pass it by. Let's go out to lunch, Rose, just you and I. We can talk over old times, and catch up on our lives."

"Out to lunch?" Rose said. "After all these years, Mary?"

"Why not?" Mary said. "It's ten minutes before noon. You do get a lunch break, don't you? I know a lovely little tearoom just around the corner on Market Street, and we could have a delicious lunch and a chat. What do you say?"

Rose shrugged. "I'll have to ask Mrs. Hedges, my superior, if it's all right. I only get 30 minutes, though, so we can't be long."

Mrs. Hedges was a woman with the posture of a ballerina and the frosty mien of a curmudgeon. She rarely smiled, and never got chummy with her staff. She agreed to Rose's request with a simple, "Be back in 30 minutes," without ever looking up from the paperwork she was doing at her desk.

At the tea room, which was full of women like Mary who oozed money and elegance, Mary ordered finger sandwiches and tea for them, folded her hands, and said: "So, Rose, how have the years been for you?"

Rose sighed. She knew very well that Mary had probably heard all about her troubles many times over. After all, Mary had written the letter years ago to Rose's father in Ireland telling him that Rose had gotten pregnant before she married Peter Morley. Mary was very connected to the Irish community in Philadelphia, and since she had always been a gossip, Rose figured she knew a lot.

"I would suppose you've heard a bit about me, Mary Driscoll."

"No, I have not," Mary said. "It may surprise you, but Philadelphia is a big enough place that a person can disappear from sight. You don't keep in touch with anyone I know. Of course, we travel in different circles now." It was another show of Mary's status, but Rose ignored it.

"I can understand why you might feel shy about telling me anything," Mary said. "I know I was the cause of some trouble for you when I wrote that letter to your father. Sorry I am for it now, Rose. I was just a broth of a girl, you understand, and I was angry at you for making me lose my position with the Lancasters."

"You stole from Mrs. Lancaster, Mary."

"That I did, and it was wrong," Mary said. "I made a mistake or two in my youth, I am ashamed to say. You'll get no argument from me about the right or wrong of it. It's just, I wanted something better than what we had in Ireland, Rose, and I didn't know how to get it. And when I lost my position, well, it was like a death sentence. No proper lady would hire me after that, and I thought I'd have to go back to the old country and live in shame for the rest of my life. Can you see how it would make me a bit mad?"

Rose said nothing.

Mary smiled. "Ah, well, I know, there's no use in digging up old grievances. Let the past be dead and buried, I say. I've come a long way since then, as you can see."

"You look well, Mary."

Mary smiled at the compliment, pleased as could be. "It's just a bit o' luck, I suppose. I had a hard time of it those first few years, Rose. I don't want to talk about all the things I did to keep body and soul together. I found myself living a desperate life, with a hard crowd of people."

She took a sip of her tea, holding her finger aloft like a lady, and then putting her cup down on the saucer daintily. "Those were bad years, Rose. I often wondered what was going to happen to me, where I'd fetch up. After ten years of living hand to mouth, with some days not enough food to keep a field mouse alive, God smiled on me and I found a respectable position. I was hired at the seminary, of all places, to be a housekeeper for the priests who taught there! I got a nice, clean room, three square meals a day, and all the confessions my soul could handle."

"I never knew you to be a religious woman, Mary," Rose said. "I well remember how you wouldn't get out of bed on Sunday mornings to go to Mass with me."

Mary laughed. "Oh, I was a pagan in those days, Rose, to be sure. I couldn't be bothered with priests and all their fussing. A few years of hunger will change a woman's mind, though. Another year and I'd have surely become a nun, if they'd have taken me." She laughed in her jolly way, and Rose couldn't help but smile.

"A nun!" Rose said. "I have a hard time seeing you in a nun's habit. You always liked fine clothes, Mary."

"Lucky for me it didn't happen," Mary said, winking. "I was saved by the priests, and I showed them my gratitude by being the best housekeeper they ever had. It was a happy time for me, and I made a lot of good friends among the clergy. And all the good that's happened to me since is a result of my time at the St. Charles Seminary."

"You don't mean to say you're still working there, Mary?"

"No, Rose, I left that position years ago. I met a good Catholic man named Francis Dillon, a man who had a small bricklaying company. He was hired to work on an addition to one of the buildings at the seminary. I met him, and it was love at first sight. Oh, I don't say he lit all the candles for me, you understand, the way some others did. Francis was a quiet, simple man, but I had had enough of the other type, and I was ready for a man like him. And he has taken good care of me, I must admit." She emphasized her point by holding out her hand to show Rose the several gold rings on her fingers, including an elaborate diamond wedding ring.

"I take it he's a man of wealth," Rose said.

"Not when I met him," Mary said. "No, he was a simple bricklayer, with a half a dozen fellows working for him. But I have helped him to expand his business, so to speak. Why, today his company is one of the largest in the city for brickwork. He does all the work for the archdiocese."

"Does he now?"

"Yes," Mary said, lowering her voice conspiratorially. "It so happens that one of the young priests I met back in my seminary days was Dennis Joseph Dougherty. You've heard of him, of course? The Cardinal?"

"I've heard of him," Rose said. "They call him 'The Great Builder' because he's put up so many new churches and schools."

"To be sure," Mary said. "And my Francis' company is usually the one doing the brickwork. The Cardinal has been good to us. Why, I can't tell you how many dinners I've been to at his residence, grand affairs with many important people at them. He's a very powerful man, you know. The Mayor, the Governor, all the politicians come calling on him. They want the Catholic vote. And there's me, Mary Driscoll from Skibbereen, sitting there talking to them, like I was born to it. Can you imagine?"

"You've done very well for yourself, Mary," Rose said. "I am happy for you."

"And how about you, Rose?" Mary said. "How have things been for you? Are you still married to that handsome coachman named Peter?"

The name could still produce a stab to her chest, an ache that never quite went away. "No," Rose said. "He left me a long time ago, and he passed from this life two years ago last July. I have made my way without him for many a year now. I had three sons with him, but only one has survived. I am remarried now."

"I am sorry to hear of your hardship," Mary said. "The handsome boyos cause us so much trouble don't they? It must have been the devil of a time for you, with three sons and no husband. Did you get a divorce? You say you are remarried. How do you stand with the Church?"

Mary looked a little too eager to hear the story, and Rose felt the anger rising in her at Mary's smug face. "There was no divorce, Mary, if that's what you're asking. I had three small boys and no job when he left me, and I had no time to be thinking of anything but trying to survive. And I'll thank you for not judging me. I know it's not easy for you to do, since you're a pillar of the Church these days."

Mary's eyes widened. "But Rose, you are in a predicament. You can't receive the Eucharist--"

"I don't need any lessons in church law, Mary," Rose snapped. "I have done what I thought best. I haven't set foot in a Catholic Church in many a year, for just such a reason as that look on your face. I got that very look from priests and people in the pews, and I got sick to death of it."

"Then you don't go to church anymore, Rose Sullivan? What would your dear father think?"

"I don't care what my dear father would think. I go to a church where I'm accepted for who I am. It's my husband's church, and it's Episcopal. I'm married to Martin Lancaster. Do you remember him?"

Mary's jaw dropped.

"You don't mean to say the Martin Lancaster. . . the one who was a boy when we worked for the family. . . I always knew he had a soft spot for you, Rose, but you're not saying. . .?"

"Yes, I am saying," Rose said. "He has been a kind and gentle friend to me for so long, and now he is my husband. And I have never been happier, Mary. And now, if you will excuse me, it's time that I get back to work." She grabbed her purse, pulled a five-dollar bill out, slapped it on the table, and said, "I won't be needing any change," and walked out, with Mary staring after her open-mouthed.

CHAPTER TWO

October 31, 1936

Rose walked home along Market Street, the burnt umber sun slanting between the high buildings. There was a late October chill in the air, and a strange stillness even in the midst of the people walking home from work. The sky was going dark behind the clock on the City Hall tower, which said 5:00.

Martin would probably still be at work, meeting with a client in one of the many rooms honeycombed through the City Hall building, or perhaps sharing a table at one of the cheap restaurants nearby.

She could go visit him, of course, but she did not want to disturb him just now. She did not want to worry him with the news that she had lost her job.

She waited to cross the street at the traffic light at Broad Street, and heard a newsboy hawking papers with the latest headlines about the country's economic troubles. There was a disheveled man in a greasy black raincoat standing nearby holding a tin cup out for donations, another victim of the bad times.

And now she was part of it. After 35 years at Wanamaker's store, waiting on the rich and high-born women of Philadelphia, year after year of faithful service, she had been turned out.

"I am afraid we have no place for you anymore," Mrs. Hedges had said. "The economy is distressed, as you know. Some of our longstanding customers have had to cut back. With all the worries in Europe caused by that dreadful man Hitler, some of our

Society women are not going abroad this season, and so they do not need a new wardrobe. I have been told we are not selling enough merchandise to justify the size of our staff. You have been eliminated, Mrs. Lancaster. Your last paycheck is waiting downstairs at the Payroll Office."

And that was that. She was 74 years old, and out of a job. Her feet ached, her bones creaked, and her hearing was not what it used to be. She would like to have stayed in bed in the mornings instead of going to work, but Martin made so little money in his law practice, often not taking any fee from his destitute clients, and she needed to work just to help pay their bills.

She had served the store faithfully, and there were women who asked for her when they came to the store. She had built up relationships with them over many years, and some of them were the daughters of women she had first served. They called her "Dear Rose" and "Darling Rose" and they treated her with condescension, telling her how charming her Irish accent was. Rose knew they would never consider her their equal, but she thought it meant something that they asked for her, that she had gotten to know their life stories and had a certain familiarity with them.

"But what about my clients?" Rose had said to Mrs. Hedges.

"They will move on," the other woman said. "We must never delude ourselves, Rose, into thinking that we are anything more than servants to them. They will forget our names a week after we've left. Is there anything else?"

It was clear she wanted Rose to leave. Rose went downstairs to the Payroll Office feeling like she had been punched in the stomach. Gladys Foley, the middle-aged gossip who worked in

Payroll, handed Rose her check and said, "I think it's despicable, Rose, what they did to you. Letting you go like that."

"Ah, it's because of the hard times," Rose said. "Business is down. My clients have no money."

"Is that what they told you?" Gladys said.

"Yes, what other reason could there be?"

Gladys lowered her voice. "It has very little to do with the economy. One of your clients had to cut her staff, it's true, and she had to fire a maid who had been with her for 25 years. She knew people in the right places, this lady did, and she got her servant a job in your department. Your job. She's starting on Monday."

Rose was too stunned to speak. She simply took the check from Gladys and left.

She walked along numbly, trying to make sense of it all. She moved among the crowds like a ghost, feeling like she was lost and without a home.

Winter was coming. The news was worse every day about an economy that was moving back into Depression after things had finally started to look up last year. There was trouble in Europe, and people were actually talking about war again. She was worried about Martin, too -- he was having problems with his eyesight, and they didn't have the money for him to go to a doctor.

Oh, Paul could help them out, it was true. He was a successful businessman, running that paper mill now and living in a grand house in the suburbs. He seemed to have it all -- a beautiful wife, and two sparkling, effervescent children. The girl, Rosie, who'd been named for her, was Rose's special delight.

But something didn't seem right with Paul. The last year when Rose visited the family Paul seemed distant, even cold, towards Lucy. He was often away, busy with an expansion of his plant down on Delaware avenue, and even when he was home he was distracted, hardly listening to what Lucy or the children said to him. Rose could see the heartache in Lucy's eyes, and she worried that there was trouble between them.

It was distressing, because Rose knew she was in the twilight of her life, and she wanted her family to be happy more than ever now. When she looked in the mirror she saw an old woman looking back, and the weight of Time was on her. It was important to her to know that her family would live on after she was gone.

She had not been able to save her family in Ireland. They were all vanished now except for her sister Annie, who had gone off to Liverpool. Now all she wanted to do was keep her family in America going, to see another generation take its rightful place in the procession of Life. Her biggest fear was that something would happen to Paul's marriage, and that her grandchildren would have a tumultuous childhood the way her own children did.

Why was this life so hard? It was nothing but struggle, heartache and loss, all the way through.

She turned down a side street, preoccupied with her thoughts, and then was brought up short by the sound of a horse whinnying. She looked up to see a large black horse at the end of the street, which was really a blind alley, or a cul-de-sac, lined with brick twin homes with porches and gables, in a style that seemed very old.

The horse stood stock still, and Rose watched as its huge dark eyes stared at her. It was pitch black, with a jagged white streak running down its forehead, and its muscles rippled under its shiny coat.

It was the strangest thing, but Rose felt like she'd been on this street before. There was an air of familiarity -- had she seen those houses before? There was no activity in them -- there were no people sitting on the porches, no lights in the windows, no sign of any human beings anywhere.

And the horse -- what was familiar about it? It was strange enough to see a horse these days -- the city was noisy with cars, trucks, and buses hurrying everywhere, and the simpler days of Rose's youth, when horses pulled wagons and carriages, were gone forever.

But this horse was somehow familiar. It seemed to recognize Rose. Now it pawed the ground with its foreleg and tossed its head, seeming anxious to communicate with her.

Rose moved toward the horse, as if in a dream. She did not understand what was going on, but somehow she felt compelled to go nearer to the animal. As she walked closer she could see the horse getting agitated, even stamping its foot, and steam was coming out of its nose. Normally that would have been a signal for Rose not to approach any closer, but she kept walking, compelled by some force she did not understand.

When she was about two hundred paces away, the horse suddenly reared, then let out a scream and charged toward her. Rose could hear the hooves on the pavement, a staccato clopping sound that seemed to echo off the brick houses in the narrow, closed street like gunshots. Its eyes were focused on her with a mad intensity, and she froze, unable to get her body to move out of the way.

Then a thought came to her. She was on the same street where so many years before the horse pulling the carriage with her, Mary Driscoll, and the Lancaster children had gone berserk, and where Sean McCarthy had reentered her life when he brought the horse under control.

Was this the same horse?

No, it couldn't be. The thoughts were cascading through her head as the horse approached, and she tried to make sense of it all. How could it be the same horse?

Rose could smell the animal now, and it smelled like, like -- turf. It smelled like the turf she remembered cutting as a child in Skibbereen, the turf in the bogs outside of town, the black spongy stuff they cut out of trenches, drying it in rows in the air so they could burn it in the fireplace later. It was a deep, black, earthy smell, full of longing and memory.

The sound of the horse's hooves was ringing in Rose's ears, drowning everything else out now. She realized with cold rationality that she was going to die. It was like she was thinking of someone else's death. She saw Martin weeping next to her casket, and Paul looking shaken. She saw her grandchildren trying to understand it all, and even Mary Driscoll shedding a tear. It was like it was happening to someone else.

***

She awoke to a sort of chanting, a guttural, singsong voice that kept repeating a phrase over and over. She lay there for a few minutes trying to get her bearings, and she finally realized that she was lying in a bed near a window and there were candles burning around her. Her body felt like someone had dropped it down a well, and she groaned as she realized it hurt to move.

Then there was a hand helping her to sit up, and a cup pressed to her lips.

"Drink!," a female voice said. "It is gutt."

She drank, feeling the hot liquid burning her throat as it went down. It tasted like licorice, earth, whiskey, branches and leaves.

She choked and coughed, but the voice urged her to drink more, and she swallowed another mouthful, feeling a pleasant sensation this time as the burning liquid hit her stomach.

The hands helped her to lie back again, and the voice said, "Now you sleep some more. That is gutt. Healing happens then."

She tried to stay awake, but the woman's chanting lulled her into a dreamlike state, where she saw people from her past, including her mother. It was her mother as she had been when Rose was a child, laughing and telling her stories, reciting her poetry and singing her songs.

There was such a feeling of longing in Rose when she saw her mother, such a power calling to her. She wanted to go back, to be a child again and sit by her mother's feet while she spun her yarns about the ancient bards and the kings and queens and giants and all the other creatures who lived in the land so many centuries before. She felt the warmth of the turf fire and the way the firelight made shadows on the walls and ceiling of the little stone house, and the flecks of gold in her mother's green eyes, the way her voice got so low and hushed and then sprang up in a great wail or a shout, the children screaming with terror or laughing deliriously at her stories.

Rose was in a strange half dream, dimly aware, not knowing what if what she saw was happening outside of her or inside her head. The low, guttural voice came back from time to time, the hands lifted her up and had her drink the pungent, hot liquid, and then laid her down to sleep again.

She heard murmurings and chants, something that sounded like prayers in a different language. Was it German? It sounded throaty, old, tinged with wisdom. She didn't know what the words meant. She wondered where the voice was coming from, but her body hurt too much to move. It was better just to lie here peacefully and let the sounds and the pictures wash over her.

She didn't know how much time had passed, but then she awoke, to the sound of birds chirping in a tree outside her window. There were other sounds too, cars and trucks in a street nearby, and the pop and sizzle of bacon frying from another room.

She sat up and tried to orient herself, to make out where she was. It was a small bedroom with a dark wood dresser on the other side of the room, and she could see herself reflected in a mirror above the dresser. The furniture was old and dark, and the walls were covered with colorful designs, and Rose recognized them as Pennsylvania Dutch Hex signs. She knew this because she sometimes went to the Reading Terminal Market, where the Amish farmers sold their produce, and there was a stall where some of the women sold needlepoint and quilts, which had the signs on them.

Just then a sturdy white haired woman in a long gray dress with a white apron and a small white cap on her head, came into the room.

"So, you are up! Gutt. You will eat now."

She brought a tray with a meal of bacon, eggs, toast and coffee and set it in front of Rose in the bed. She was peremptory in her manner, practically commanding Rose to eat and drink, and Rose obeyed mutely. She was hungrier than she thought. The meal tasted delicious, and she finished it quickly.

"Where am I?" she said, finally. "What happened to me?"

"You have had a fall," the woman said. "Down in the street. You hurt your head." She touched a bandage on Rose's forehead. "You do not remember?"

"I remember the horse," Rose said. "There was a black horse that came galloping up the street at me. What was that horse doing here?"
"Horse? There was no horse." The woman looked at her with concern in her eyes. "What did you see?"

"Why, it was a big, black thing, as big as a house it seemed. It was charging right down the street at me. I thought it was going to run me over. You did not see it?"

"Ach, there are none of them here. No horses."

"But are you sure? Perhaps you did not see?"

"No horse. I was looking out the window at you. I saw you fall down, but no horse did I see."

Rose was adamant. "Well, I'm not going mad, I am sure of that. I know I saw that horse."

"You are not English, ya?" the woman said. "Your voice is different."

"I am from Ireland," Rose said.

The woman looked at her. "I know some of the stories from your land. It is a land haunted by the past, they say. What is your name?"

"Rose. Rose Lancaster. Who are you?" Rose said, rousing herself. "Where am I? I need to get back to my house. My husband will be worried about me." She suddenly realized the strangeness of being here with this woman. She wondered if the woman had stolen anything from her. She fingered the gold locket around her neck, the one that Martin had given her from the estate of his mother. It was still there.

"Yes, in gutt time. I am Jenny Miller. I am Deitsh. Pennsylvania German. I live here."

"But I thought you people lived in the farm country out west," Rose said.

Jenny smiled. "I am not like the others. Have you heard of pow-wow? No? It is a form of medicine. I learned it from my mother. It is a healing medicine, and I practice it. The others think it is witchcraft. So," she shrugged her shoulders, "I am not allowed to live among them. They shun me. But they still come to see me when they have a problem, the hypocrites! Ya, they seek me out when they need answers! I can fix problems."

The strangeness of this woman, this room, was suddenly too much for Rose to take. "I need to go." Rose pushed the tray and the covers aside. "I need to get back."

The woman grabbed her wrist. "You should not go yet. There is trouble in the air around you. You should let me say some prayers over you."

"Sure, and I don't believe in that nonsense," Rose said. "I will be fine. I thank you for taking care of me, but I must go now."

She stood up, a bit unsteadily, but she managed to keep her balance. She did not even know what time it was, but she felt she needed to leave. The business about the horse scared her, as if there were something supernatural going on.

"Let Jenny walk you home," the woman said. "You are unsteady. You may fall down again."

"No thank you," Rose said. "I can manage by myself. I must leave now."

Outside, it was a bright October day, about mid-morning, Rose judged. She must have spent the night in Jenny's house. Martin would be worried, and she'd have quite a story to tell him.

She shivered as she walked away, feeling Jenny's eyes on her. She turned once and saw the woman standing in the front of her house, looking after her.

CHAPTER THREE

January 20, 1937

"You're heading for disaster, Mister Morley," the accountant had said. He was a little man named Arthur Peabody with a prim little mustache and a fringe of brown hair around his bald head, and Paul hated him. He was the head bookkeeper for Duncan Paper Industries, and as such he was always bringing Paul Morley bad news.

Paul realized that somebody had to keep track of the dollars and cents, but it was so earthbound and boring, really. All this Peabody fellow ever seemed to know how to do was say "No".

He was sitting across from Paul in the conference room that Paul had had redesigned, at the new polished mahogany conference table. Paul had been on a spending spree, and this was just one of his projects. There was also the expansion of the paper mill, the purchase of the latest equipment for turning pulp into paper, the new advertising campaign he had launched, and the new employees he had added.

Paul could look out the window right past Peabody's head and see the orange cranes against the sky, and he could hear the sounds of the mechanized equipment that was building the new facility. It was a cathedral to industry he was building, a mighty monument to his drive, a powerful affirmation of his intelligence and energy and vision.

The only problem was, as Peabody kept reminding him, he had picked the wrong time to expand.

"As you know, Mr. Morley, the country is going through hard times," Peabody would say, his little mustache twitching, his face flushing pink with emotion. "Our sales are down compared to five years ago. This is not the time to spend money on an expansion."

Paul had ignored him, convinced the little fussbudget was wrong.

After all, who would know best about how to run a company, Peabody or him? He was Paul Morley, wasn't he? He had come to work at this place when he was just a boy, and worked his way up the ladder to president. He'd married the owner's pretty daughter, expanded the product line, developed new markets, and now he owned the place down to the last paper clip. Old George Campbell had died ten years ago and left the company to Paul, and he'd built a dynamo ever since. He lived in a world of country clubs and fast cars and beautiful men and women, and he fit in so well -- even speaking with just the hint of an English accent -- that you would have thought he was born to it.

It was the reward for all his hard work, although it never seemed to satisfy the hunger inside him, the hunger to excel, to climb ever higher and get ever further away from his shabby beginnings. He wanted to get as far away from his childhood as possible, far away from the seedy rooming houses and the taunts of the schoolchildren, calling him names because of his absent father.

He still awoke at night in a sweat sometimes, the fear clutching him, the feeling of being trapped in a life he couldn't control, the longing for the father who was never there, the hunger in his stomach from not having enough to eat. He had been running from it his whole life and he wanted to put as much distance as possible between himself and the skinny, starving little boy whose father left him.

"Mr. Morley, I've been speaking to you."

It was Peabody, looking at him disapprovingly as if he were a teacher reprimanding a little boy daydreaming in class. "Can we please go over these numbers? It took me all week to prepare them, and I think it's important for you to see this."

"Why certainly, Peabody old man. Proceed, proceed." Paul folded his hands and waited for the bad news.

Peabody shuffled his papers and began talking, displaying charts with sales figures, cost increases, projections, cash flow predictions, all of it painting a bigger picture of gloom and desperation with each new chart.

Finally, he sat back in his chair, the papers spread out in front of Paul, and said: "The plain fact is our markets have dried up. Almost a third of the companies we sold to ten years ago have gone out of business. We've replaced very few of them with new customers, Mr. Morley. The business climate in this country is just abysmal, and has been since the stock market crash in '29. I don't see any relief in sight, either. Add to that the cost of this building spree you've been on, and this company is heading for a big fall."

He sat there with his arms folded across his chest, as if he were a grocery clerk waiting for a small boy to explain why he had stolen an apple from the fruit stand.

"Not to worry, Peabody," Paul said. "Not to worry. Everything will be fine, old man. It's just a momentary disturbance. The country is going through a bit of a rough patch, but things will turn out right. It's the fault of that man in the White House, you know, that blasted Roosevelt. It baffles me how he could get reelected after the mischief he did in his first term. Why, the old rascal is getting sworn in for another term at this very moment! Well, at least we have the satisfaction of knowing he can't run again in four years. We'll be rid of the blasted socialist then, and the country can get back to the business of private industry, what made us great in the first place."

"But you can't wait four years for a savior," Peabody said, his mustache twitching nervously. "By then this company will be out of business, Mr. Morley, I guarantee it. We need a solution quicker than that."

"Agreed," Paul said. "I am working on that. It will all turn out fine, Peabody, I assure you. This company will not only survive, it will thrive. Better days are coming!" He slapped the table for emphasis, causing Peabody to adjust his glasses.

"Those are encouraging words, Mr. Morley," Peabody said, finally. "But, may I ask what your plan is? Because the banks certainly aren't lending any money, so you won't get any cash from them. I'd like to know where you're going to get the money to make up for the shortfall I see coming very soon."

"Oh, that's for me to know and you to find out, isn't it?" Paul said, winking. He stood up abruptly. "It's been good chatting with you, Peabody, but I have an important dinner to go to and I must cut this meeting short."

"But Mr. Morley," Peabody said. "I waited a week to get this meeting with you. I prepared all these reports. Really, this is a matter you need to address immediately. I am afraid for the future of this company. . ."

"Now, don't you worry yourself, old man," Paul said, gathering the papers up and stuffing them in Peabody's black leather briefcase. "It's not worth losing sleep over. I'll have this place running like a top again, I promise you. Just leave it to old Paul Morley, everything will turn out right. Now, if you'll excuse me, I really must go." He put his hand under Peabody's elbow and helped the little man to his feet, then ushered him toward the door.

"But, Mr. Morley, I think we should discuss this further," Peabody spluttered, his face crimson and his mustache twitching. "This is highly irregular. I mean--"

"Yes, yes," Paul said. "We will have to schedule another meeting sometime next week. Just check with my secretary, will you? There's a good man." He pushed Peabody out the door and closed it firmly.

He went over to the window and looked out at the construction site again. It made him feel powerful to look at all that work going on because of him, because of the force of his will. A year ago there had been nothing there but an old broken down warehouse, and now it was a hive of activity, men and machines working all day long to create something that he had willed into existence.

What did he care about a momentary downturn in the economy? It would not stand in his way. It was all due to the socialist in the White House anyway, that scoundrel Franklin Roosevelt, who was a traitor to his class. The man seemed determined to wreck everything that made this country great. He was pro-Labor and anti-business, that was certain, and he did nothing but raise taxes and expand the government, reaching its hands into more and more of the lives of honest businesspeople.

In Paul's view the country had been run for years by people who knew best, a class of people who were bred to make decisions and run things efficiently, a bright and happy class who lived a shining life in their mansions and their cities far above the lives of the common folk. They were the best and the brightest, and they lived a far different life than others, a more vivid, happy life. They were set apart from the common herd, and you had to be born into their world.

Once in awhile, though, there were people who gained admission through their own intelligence, hard work, and luck, and he was one of them. He had become a part of them, through learning the right manners and the right way of speaking and the right way of behaving, through his gift for conversation, for making the sale, which earned him enough money so the important people paid attention to him. Money was his ticket to admission, and through that he met all the right people. He had gained admittance to the club, and he was confident that things would turn out for the best. These people always took care of their own, didn't they?

He would find that out soon, when he approached them for the money to keep his company afloat.

That thought brought him back to reality. He pulled his gold watch out of his vest pocket and saw that it was 4:00. He'd better get going if he was going to drive home and get ready in time for the dinner party he was invited to tonight. He snapped the watch shut, put it in his pocket, and went out to the front office, where his receptionist, a handsome young woman named Gladys Worthington, was sitting. Most companies did not believe in hiring women for office work but Paul knew the value of having a pretty woman at the front desk. It made his suppliers a lot happier to sit across from Gladys while they waited to see him about overdue bills.

"I'll be leaving now, Gladys," he said. "I have to drive home and get ready for a big shindig tonight."

"But Mr. Morley," she said. "There are people waiting to see you." She pointed to two men sitting on the plush red leather chairs across the spacious reception room from her desk. Paul recognized them as wood pulp suppliers from Canada to whom he owed money.

"Oh, I quite forgot about them," he said, under his breath. "Tell them to come back tomorrow."

"But they've been waiting for hours," she whispered. "I don't think they'll like that."

"Nonsense," he said. "They just need a little persuasion." He strode over to the two men, who rose to meet him. They were dressed in an overabundance of clothing for this time of year, with brown wool suits and bulky winter coats and black fedoras and gloves.

"Hello, gentlemen," Paul said. "I'm sorry I made you wait. Important meeting with my bookkeeping fellow."

"Well, we were getting a little tired of cooling our heels," the larger of the two said. "Although the scenery was terrific." He pointed at Gladys, who pretended not to notice.

"Yes, I know what you mean," Paul said, winking. "Makes things a lot more pleasant, doesn't it?"

They giggled like schoolboys, and Paul knew he had them in his back pocket. He put his arms around them and talked in a conspiratorial tone. "You know, I can probably get a date for you two with Gladys and one of her friends. She has some astoundingly beautiful friends, and I know she'd be just delighted to go out for drinks with you boys tonight. It would be my pleasure, since I'm going to have to cancel our meeting today. Something terribly important has come up, and I'll have to see you tomorrow instead."

Their faces fell.

"What do you mean?" the large one said.

"Yes, this is the second time you've put us off," the small one said. He was standing with his hands on his hips, and he looked like he was ready for a fight. "We're not fools, you know. You're late with your payments, and we won't be trifled with. We demand to speak with you now, damn it, Morley!"

Paul put his finger to his lips and said, "Shh, please fellows, don't be rude in front of Gladys. You'll get her upset, and then she won't want to go out with you. Now, I know you must be a bit irritated to have me cancel yet another meeting, but I just can't get out of this engagement tonight. I promise I'll make it up to you. Listen, just to show you what a good sport I am, I'll pay for your evening. I'll have Gladys make a reservation at the best chop house in town, and you can eat and drink to your heart's content. Then, there are a few nightclubs the girls can show you, and I'm sure you'll have a good time there. After that, who knows?" He winked at them again, and nudged the large one in the ribs, and he knew the deal was done.

"Aw, I guess we could wait another day," the large man said. "What do you say, Aidan? We'll just make up some excuse for the office. We've done it before and they never seemed to mind."

"I don't like it," the little man said. "It's not proper; we're here to collect a business debt. Besides, if Mr. Morley can pay for a night on the town for us, why can't he just write us a check for what's owed to our company?"

"And that's exactly what I intend to do," Paul said, clapping him on the shoulder. "As soon as I do a little work behind the scenes. I have some business deals that are about to come to fruition, as it were, and by tomorrow I should have all the funds in hand to pay you boys current. The fact is, I'll be working on all those arrangements tonight, you see. It'll all work out, I promise you. Now, what do you say to a night out on the town, eh?" He smiled at Gladys, who responded by flashing her teeth in a brilliant smile.

"Oh, all right," the small man said. "I suppose we can wait one more day. We've waited all this time, after all."

"Good!" Paul said. "You won't regret it."

CHAPTER FOUR

May, 1937

"You are not well, Mr. Lancaster." She had white hair tied up in a bun under her white cotton cap, but her face was strangely unlined for a woman who was supposed to be in her 60s. Her green eyes were like specks in her face, with a glint of mischief in them. Martin was sitting across from her at a long table in one of the anterooms near the criminal court in City Hall, trying to interview her prior to her hearing later in the afternoon.

"Now, Jenny, don't start practicing that witchery on me," Martin said. "That's what got you in trouble in the first place. We're all sober citizens in this city, and we don't believe in all that hocus pocus stuff."

"It's not hocus pocus," she said, drawing her shawl around her with a show of dignity. "I practice pow wow medicine. I see things. Things that other people do not see. I know when bad is going to happen, and I know the prayers to get rid of spells." She pointed disdainfully to Martin's open law book on the table. "It is as real as the words in that book."

"Well, that's not what the DA's office says. They say you're running a gypsy operation that's bilking poor people out of their money."

"Fools," she said, waving her hand dismissively. "You English are small minded fools. I am no gypsy. It is real, what I do, not false. People pay me because I do them gutt, I help them. I am not a carnival faker. I do not take money and pretend."

Martin felt sorry for her, in a way. He knew she'd been raised Pennsylvania Dutch, but the fact that she was living in city, so far from Lancaster County where her people lived, meant that she was an outcast, someone they shunned. The Germans came into town to do their business, selling their produce at the farmer's markets, but they left as soon as it was done. They regarded the city as a place of sin, and they did not want to spend any more time than necessary in it.

They were a tight knit group, but when one of them transgressed their beliefs, the person was cast out, shunned, forever cut off from the comforts of family and friends. They would do it for various reasons, but Martin figured with Jenny it was because they thought she was a witch. She was an odd one, to be sure, with a strange way of looking right through you, and given to sudden pronouncements and twitches of her head. She played the part of a seer very well, he thought, and she apparently had something of a following. The times were uncertain, though, and people were looking for something to hold on to, an explanation for all the troubles the world was going through. Some people found that explanation in politics, some in religion, and some in visits to seers and mediums like Jenny. Martin didn't begrudge them that, and if he had his way he'd leave people like Jenny alone to ply their trade, but the DA's office didn't see it that way.

"The DA is up for reelection," Martin said. "He's looking to make some points with voters, and he's got the police commissioner pushing the vice squad to work overtime these days. It's easy for them to haul folks like you in and make a statement that they're tough on crime. I'll see what I can do to get these charges dismissed, but you should probably find another line of work."

"I have nothing to pay you with," she said. "No money."

"Really? Where's all the money the police say you took in? They found some pocket money, but they say you should have had much more, for all the clients you have."

She looked stricken. "I send it all to my son in Emmaus. He lost his leg in an accident, and he has not been right since. He cannot farm anymore. His mind is no gutt." She pointed to her head. "I send him money to help him out."

"I guess your powers can't help him, then?" Martin said.

She shrugged. "I do not benefit from my gift. That is the way it is, always." She peered at him again, examining him closely. "You are not well. Your eyes? You do not see so well."

Martin chuckled. "I don't know how you guessed that, but you're right. I suppose you saw me squinting at my paperwork. The old lamps are going a bit dim, but I'll be all right."

She did not smile at his joke. "You have a heart problem. Your heart is getting worn out."

It was unnerving, the way she was staring, and it rattled him. Martin had seen too much of the underbelly of life in his work in the criminal justice system and he had a healthy skepticism about much of what his clients told him, but something about this woman stopped him in his tracks. His mother and father had died of heart attacks, and they both had been only a few years older than he was now.

He was surprised to hear the words coming from his mouth, but he whispered, "How much time do I have left?"

She did not hesitate. "Six years."

He swallowed hard. He had been worried lately about his death. He felt urgings, intuitions, that his days were numbered. What worried him most was that he had not put enough money away for Rose to live on if something should happen to him. He had been careless with money, the way people who grow up rich often are, and he had spent his days helping clients who sometimes paid him and sometimes didn't.

There was no money left from his family. The family's fortunes had changed dramatically from the days of the big house in Chestnut Hill. Twenty years ago his father had quarreled with his law partners and left the firm, then made some bad investments, then got tuberculosis and spent thousands of dollars on trips to sanatoriums in Europe before he died. By the time Martin's mother had died five years ago, the little money she had to live on was wiped out in the stock market crash, and there was hardly anything of value left in her estate.

"Well, I sincerely hope you're wrong," Martin said, with his best show of cheeriness. "If I croak in six years I'll be leaving this earth as a poorer man than when I started out. Of course, they say that's the sign of a life well lived, isn't it? It means you enjoyed your money rather than hoarded it."

"I will say some prayers for you," Jenny said.

"Please do," Martin said, grinning. "Please do. Nothing wrong with prayer."

"You have a wife?" she said, suddenly. "What is her name?"

"Now, listen, Jenny," he said. "I'm the one who's supposed to be asking the questions here. We don't need to delve into my personal details."

She was looking at him with those inquisitive eyes, blinking and tilting her head. "What is her name, please?"

"Rose. Her name is Rose."

She looked shaken. Her lip twitched, and her fingers gripped the table. "She was at my house."

"What? What are you talking about? I doubt my wife has ever met you."

She shook her head. "Ya, she was at my house. Last Fall, around the time of the new moon. She collapsed in my street, and I brought her home and said my prayers, my words, and she woke up. She has great sadness around her."

"Now, Jenny," Martin said. "I really don't believe--"

"She is a tall woman with white hair and eyes like the sea, and she was wearing a gold locket around her neck." She touched her neck with her fingertips. "It was shaped like a heart."

Martin drew in his breath. It was the locket from his mother, the one he had given to Rose years ago. He was stunned, and for a moment or two he could not speak.

"She didn't come home one night last October," he said. "I was worried sick about her, and I called all the hospitals in the city. She told me she was knocked unconscious by a horse, and some kind women took care of her. Was that you?"

Jenny shook her head yes.

"Thank you," he said. "I am grateful for what you did for her." Suddenly he had to know. "Is she going to be all right? What else do you see?" He felt like the ground was shaky under his feet. If anything happened to Rose he could not go on, he knew that.

"She is haunted by the past," Jenny said. "She carries it around with her always. She survives, though. She is tough, like old shoe leather. Her son, though, he is heading for a fall."

"Paul?" Martin said. "That's not possible. He's a successful businessman, with a beautiful wife and two handsome children. Why, he's one of the few people I know who hasn't been affected by this blasted Depression. The man is an absolute genius at business."

"There is a hateful spirit around him," Jenny said. "Cold, bitter, evil." She drew her shawl around her as if she'd been hit with a blast of icy air. "He is weak. . ." suddenly her hand shot out, and she clutched Martin's wrist. "You must speak to him. Tell him not to get mixed up with that other man."

"What other man?" Martin said. "I need more information than that, Jenny."

She put her hand to her eyes and shook her head. "I do not know. . . it is fading. . . I cannot see. . ."

Martin shook his head. "I'm not sure, Jenny. Some of what you say seems on the mark, but the rest of it. . ." his voice trailed off. She had been right about the locket though. He couldn't deny that. What if she was right about Paul?

"What's going to happen to him?" he said, leaning forward and lowering his voice. "Can you give me any more details?"

"No," she said abruptly. "I see what I see, and sometimes it is cloudier than other times. I cannot see more. You should talk to him, though."

"That I will do," Martin said. "I can see you are a valuable person to know, Jenny. I hope you will tell me if you get any more feelings about my loved ones. I will handle your legal matters for free, if you'll let me come and visit from time to time."

"Ya," Jenny said. "That would be gut."

Martin had a lot to think about after that, not least of which was how to tell Paul that a Pennsylvania Dutch seer had warned that he was in trouble. I don't know how that's going to sound, he thought. He'll probably think I'm crazy and kick me out of his office.

CHAPTER FIVE

June, 1937

My Dearest Brother Edward,

If this letter reaches you, I pray that you take the time to read it. Please do not tear it up and throw it away, since it contains the deepest hopes and longings of your sister Edith. I miss you all very much, and I long to hear from you again.

I hope this letter finds you and your family in good health. It has been many years since we have had any contact, and I am writing to the last address I had for you. In such troubled times as these it is very possible that you have moved, and this letter will not reach you. I dearly hope that by the grace of God it does reach you, for I worry constantly about you and the rest of the family, and I should like to hear how you are doing. The newspapers here are full of reports about the worsening situation in Europe, and some people in America are saying there could be war before long.

I can scarcely believe that our dear England could be facing another war, only a generation since the last one. It worries me very much, and I think often of our family and relatives, wondering how everyone is doing. There were many times that I thought of moving back to England the way you did years ago, because I missed my homeland so deeply, but perhaps it is for the best that I never did. I feel safer here in America, far away from the storms in Europe.

I know we have not spoken in many years, because you and the others cut off contact with me when I married that Irishman James Francis. It is a wound that still hurts me, and I wish more than ever that we could heal it. I have never gotten over the loss of my dear family in England.

It hurts even more because I have a family myself that you have never met. I have a son and daughter, John and Mercy, and they are all grown up with busy lives of their own. We have been through a lot, and there is so much I could tell you. I will simply say that my husband James died two years ago, and that I live alone now in Philadelphia.

It was a troubled marriage, to be quite honest. It had nothing to do with his social station; he was a lively, intelligent man who could talk to anyone, and he fit in easily wherever he went. However, he was not an honest man, and he deceived me about some important things. It turned out that he was married before and did not bother to get a divorce. Indeed, he had children from this marriage also. He concealed his first marriage from me, and I only found out about it by happenstance.

This was a heavy blow to bear, and I never really recovered from it. James and I separated, and although he never left my life completely, things were not the same between us. Things are never completely black and white in matters of the heart, however, are they? I still loved him very much, even though this terrible thing happened between us. I can even say that I love him still, and I miss him now that he is gone.

It has warped my children's lives in many subtle ways. Mercy, my daughter, seems ever to have problems with the men in her lives. I don't think she can ever really trust a man completely. John, my son, has no direction in his life, and drifts from one thing to the next. Neither one of them has much time for me, I am afraid. They are not unkind to me, but they seem to associate me with the horrible time when their father betrayed us, and they do not want to be reminded of it, I suppose.

I have met the woman that James was married to before. I met her on the day of his funeral. She is a lovely woman, and I have no hard feelings toward her. In fact, I have often thought in the last few years that I would like to meet her and tell her something about James that might give her an understanding of the torment he was living with. I know some things about him that might give her peace. We all struggle to make the right choices in life, but we often stumble and fall, don't we?

I have made do, muddling along as best I could. I turned 60 years old this year, and I live in a small apartment in the city. I have very little money saved, so I must work to pay my bills. I found a job in a little pharmacy and five and dime store in my neighborhood, which in the Jewish section. Mr. Levin, the owner of the store, treats me very well. He is an immigrant from Germany, and he is very worried about his family over there. The news is very bad, as you know, for Jews in that country, and he is trying to get his people to leave. He lets me read some of the letters they send him, and they are always full of the most disturbing stories.

I do not understand why there is so much hate in the world. There are people even here in America who are blaming the Jews for the world's problems, and it is terrible to witness. Some days when I come to work there are swastikas drawn in chalk on the sidewalk outside the premises, and people have left leaflets in the store with the most horrid cartoons and stories about Jews.

I know it distresses Mr. Levin, but he tries not to talk about it. I see the worry in his face about his family in Germany, though. Some of them write letters and tell him this will all blow over, but he *doesn't believe them. He has only one family member here, a nephew of 17 named Avram, and the boy is a wounded soul that Mr. Levin feels responsible for.*

I have become fond of Mr. Levin, and we go out to dinner sometimes. We talk over our troubles, and we make each other laugh. It is a way of staving off the loneliness.

Are you surprised at this, Edward? I know people from our social station were not expected to consort on an intimate basis with Jews, and in fact I don't think we knew any Jewish people growing up. I suppose I am breaking some rule by doing this, but then I broke the rules many years ago when I married James, didn't I? Shouldn't we be past all that? I am a 60-year-old woman, and Simon Levin is two years older than me. Is it so wrong for two people of our age to find some comfort in each other in this upside down world?

Indeed, sometimes it seems as if the world has gone crazy. Do you remember our childhood? Things were so peaceful then. I still remember Queen Victoria's Golden Jubilee, when I was ten years old, and how we cheered as the procession with her passed on its way to Westminster Abbey for the ceremony. Do you remember the Indian cavalry, how they looked in their red and black uniforms, riding on their magnificent horses? Ah, what a sight it was, with the horses bobbing their heads and the sun glinting off the gold on their harnesses. Father put me on his shoulders, and I got a good look as the Queen passed by. She looked glorious, serene and majestic. Our country was atop the world back then, and there was nothing to fear. I don't believe I ever had an anxious moment in my whole childhood. Do you remember? It was idyllic.

The world seemed a safe place, and our lives were predictable. I thought I would marry and have a little house on the outskirts of London, and spend my time raising my children and doing some charity work perhaps.

Ah, but Life had some surprises in store for me! I did not realize how things could change so swiftly. I came across the ocean to this young and impetuous country, and I met a man who changed my life. I had some years of wild happiness with him, but also crushing sadness. He could touch your heart with his singing voice, and then sting you with his betrayals. The years when we were happy, though, were the best ones of my life.

And then everything changed. I discovered his treachery just before the First Great War, and from that day it has seemed like the world has never been the same. My life was difficult, to be sure, but I also worried every day about all of you in England. I prayed every day that you would survive, and I corresponded with Mother in secret to hear the news about you all. She did not tell any of you about this, I know, but it was a godsend to me to be able to hear what was happening to my family, even though her letters were few. When the war ended I gave thanks to God, but I was sad to hear of cousins and uncles who had died. And when Father died soon after I was heartbroken, especially because I knew I was not welcome at the funeral. When Mother died suddenly in 1925 I did not even hear about it until I sent a telegram to Aunt Eunice after my letters to mother had gone unanswered for a year. Imagine, Edward -- my mother had been dead and buried for a full year before I even knew about it! To read those words in a telegram was a wrenching moment for me.

It is not right to be cut off like this. The older I get the more I realize that family is the most important thing.

In a strange way, family is the reason why I never came back to England; my two children, who are so dear to me, feel that this is their home, and I could never leave them. I feel pulled in two directions, though, because I cannot forget my family over there. I worry about you all, and I hope this war that is predicted never happens.

Will you please write back and tell me how you are? I wake up at night sometimes and wonder if you are even alive, if any of my family is still alive. It would be a hard thing to take if my family had all died and I did not know it. It is the position that Simon Levin finds himself in, and he has urged me to contact you simply because he knows how wrenching it is to be in a state of uncertainty about one's family.

Even if you are still alive, if the situation gets worse in Europe you could be in danger. I would like to know how you all are, to stay current with these momentous events.

This is not a time for harboring old grudges and complaints, or for making judgments based on old prejudices. I listen to President Roosevelt's radio broadcasts, and I hear the note of warning in his voice. He is trying to alert us all that we may be in for a very rough time ahead. In such a time as this, we must realize what is truly important, Edward. Our family ties are what matters most. Please write back, and tell me how you are.

Your sister,

Edith

CHAPTER SIX

July, 1937

Paul drove the Packard along River Road in Bucks County, listening to the purr of its engine with satisfaction. The sun was getting low in the sky and its rays turned the Delaware River to molten gold.

He was lost in thought, letting the moment wash over him as Lucy sat silent next to him. This was an important evening for him, and for his company. He was going to a party at the house of Basil St. James, a man whose family owned a distillery in Kentucky, a share of a publishing company in Manhattan, and various other businesses. St. James lived on an estate nestled next to the river near New Hope, where he raised horses and kept a herd of Scottish highland cattle. As Paul approached the house, cascading in tiers on a hill that overlooked the river, he marveled at its beauty.

Coming up the long driveway, the house loomed like some modernist fairy tale castle, and Paul could see a white tent set up on a terrace and people in evening dress milling near a stage where a dance band in white tuxedos played the latest jazz music. Japanese paper lanterns gave a soft rainbow glow to everything.

"What a place!" Paul exclaimed, as he parked the car.

But Lucy only shrugged and said: "It's a bit too much for my taste."

A coldness had grown between them, a resentment that Paul could not understand. She told him she did not like the people he was associating with now, that they were all shallow, self-absorbed, and even dangerous in some of their views, and she made it clear she did not want to be around them. Paul was resentful that she felt this way, because he saw himself as simply striving to make something better for his family than what he had growing up. "These are the people who run things," he said. "They are the upper tier, and we've made it through their front door. We get invited to their parties, we're allowed to join their clubs. Isn't that a good thing?"

"I don't trust any of them," she said. "They'd abandon their own mother if she was holding them back. And have you listened to them? They have the most alarming views, Paul. Most of them are fervent supporters of that madman Hitler in Germany. They believe in racial purity, all that hideous Aryan philosophy. They look down on most other people in the world, don't you see that?"

"I don't believe it. They are simply used to running things, and they know best. They've been to all the best schools, Lucy. They were bred to this life."

"Yes, and that's why they will never accept us. We're different from them. My father's father was a miner in Scotland. Your mother was a servant for the rich. They will never see us as equal to them, Paul, never."

He did not understand why she couldn't see his point of view. It was a great thing to be counted among these people's friends. It was like a dream come true. He had never really believed he was worth very much, never in his heart believed that he amounted to very much even when his accomplishments piled up, when he had one success after another in the world of business. He had never felt like he made it, like he reached the top of the mountain, like he belonged anywhere, until he was finally accepted by these people, the ones who mattered, the ones who counted.

Lucy couldn't understand that, and it had caused a problem between them. He was spending more and more time away from her, busy with all his projects at work, busy with social events and club meetings and a whirlwind of activity. He got home late at night sometimes, smelling of whiskey and cigars, and she did not bother to wake up when he slipped into the bed next to her.

And there were other things taking up his attention. The women were beautiful in this world, he discovered. When he was a boy his father had taken him to work several times, letting him ride next to him in the coach when he took the Lancasters to their dinner parties, and he had been intoxicated by the women in their fancy gowns of satin and lace and their perfumes and their soft, musical voices. They seemed to be creatures from another world, too lovely to be a part of the grubby, starving world he lived in, and he was in awe of them. He remembered sitting outside of a mansion in the coach as his father waited to pick his charges up, and the music of a piano and violin floated through the night air, the women's soft forms silhouetted against the gaslight through the great windows of a ballroom, their laughter like the tinkling of faraway bells, or the whisper of angels' wings. It was a world he never thought he'd ever gain entry to, but now, miracle of miracles, he was inside the door.

And this party was going to seal his fate. For a while now he had been cultivating a friendship with Basil St. James, this man who moved gracefully in the mysterious world of money and power.

He was a man who seemed to know everyone who counted, and Paul, being a good businessperson, instinctively knew he had to become his friend. St. James was a middle-aged man with a full head of blonde wavy hair, an aquiline nose and a ready smile. He seemed always to be ready for a game of golf or tennis, but Paul could tell he had a sharp mind and a keen sense for profit in every situation.

St. James greeted Paul and Lucy at the door of his mansion, and welcomed them with a warm show of heartiness.

"Paul, old man, good to see you," he said. "And this is your lovely wife, Lucy? Charmed." He kissed Lucy on the cheek, then turned to a woman by his side, and said, "This is my wife Emily."

"So nice to meet you," Emily said, flashing a row of brilliant white teeth. "Would you like a drink? Let me show you to the bar. I have the most amazing man back there who can mix up just about anything you desire. Come." She took Lucy by the arm and escorted her away.

"We'll get a drink from one of the waiters," Basil said. "But first come with me, Paul, I want you to meet a friend of mine."

He took Paul through one elegant room after another, and then through a long corridor at the back of the house and out onto the terrace overlooking the Delaware River. There was a couple chatting off to the side, away from the main group of partygoers, and Paul was immediately aware of nothing else in the universe but the woman.

She had corn silk blonde hair pulled back in a bun, and she looked like a Nordic goddess. She had high cheekbones, milk white skin, and eyes like sapphires. She was wearing a long, silvery, figure-hugging gown and she seemed lit from within. She radiated an air of command, but also a vulnerability in the lips, a softness, that was captivating. Paul was dimly aware that Basil was introducing him, and he heard the name "Hans Guenther" and then "Trudy Guenther". She held out her hand and Paul took it. It had a cold heat coming from it.

He realized they were waiting for him to speak, and he stammered out some pleasantry about Basil not telling him he had such a lovely view of the river, and they all laughed and then Basil called a waiter over and they got drinks and Paul suddenly could think of nothing else but how he could arrange to be alone with this woman.

He had to force himself to talk to Hans, because he knew Basil had a purpose in introducing him to the man. He had told Basil he was looking for someone to put some money into his company, and Basil had promised to introduce him to a man who could help him out. That man was Hans.

Basil apparently realized that Paul was losing his bearings around this striking woman, so he said, "Now, Trudy, I'd like to steal your husband for a moment or two. He and Paul need to have a boring conversation about business, and I'm sure you'd rather listen to the orchestra or have some of the food my chef has prepared. Oh, there are the Andersons over there -- have you met them?"

He called a man and woman over and introduced them as Alan and Betty Anderson, of Villanova. Alan served on the board of directors of the Pennsylvania Railroad, Basil mentioned, and he wondered if they'd show Trudy the view down by the dock for a bit while he talked a little business with Hans and Paul? They took Trudy away and Basil led the way back into the house, with Paul and Hans following.

Basil took them through more rooms of his house, culminating in a long corridor that opened into an oak-paneled library with a stone fireplace at one end of it.

Basil sat them down in red leather chairs by the fireplace, and he poured glasses of scotch from a decanter on the side of his desk. Paul took a sip and enjoyed the mellow burn of the fine scotch as it went down.

"Now, I'll leave you two fellows to your own devices," Basil said. "I have a party to host, and my wife will be wondering where I ran off to. Make yourselves at home, and don't hesitate to dip into that scotch as much as you like."

He slipped out of the room, closing the door behind him.

"So," Hans said, folding his hands in front of him. "Basil says you are looking for someone to do business with." He was a stocky man with a wrestler's build, a bristly auburn mustache and rust colored hair brushed straight back. He smiled, but his small blue eyes looked hard and cold.

"I see you believe in getting straight to the point," Paul said.

"There is no time like the present," Hans said. "You are in need of money, I understand?" His accent was American but his speech rhythms had the ring of Germany in them, as if he had lived in America for years but had never quite gotten rid of the martial cadences of his birthplace.

"Oh, that," Paul said. "We've hit a bump in the road, like a lot of other concerns these days. It's got more to do with that man Roosevelt's policies than anything else, I'd say. As a matter of fact, I'm expanding. Building a brand new facility down on the river, with all the latest equipment. We'll have that place humming with activity within the year, and we'll be back on top."

The other man looked at him like he was a fly under a microscope. "Interesting," he said. "I have done a little research on your company, Mr. Morley, and it does not seem like this is a 'bump in the road', as you call it. It looks to me like you have overextended yourself with this ambitious building campaign, and you are in danger of having your company go bankrupt if you don't get more cash soon."

Paul felt the blood rising to his cheeks. "Now see here, I told you, it's a temporary situation. I've worked at Duncan Paper since I was a boy, and we've had 13 years in a row of rising sales since I took over the operation. Why, it's only been in the last year or so that we've had a bit of a downturn. I have no doubt that when we get this building project all finished --"

"Stop!" Hans said, pounding his hand on the arm of the chair. "This is nonsense! You did a stupid thing, expanding your company when the country is doing so poorly. I know for a fact that you owe your wood suppliers in Canada in the millions of dollars, and you have been very late with your payments. You will not have that building finished in time to save you, if you don't get some cash right away.

"Now let's deal in facts, shall we?" he continued, in a lower, measured voice. "I have money. I am prepared to lend you some of that money at very favorable rates. Much better rates than you could get from a bank, if you were even able to find a bank these days that would make a loan to you. I am able to raise some additional money from like-minded men, and I can give you $5 million, which should be enough to help you finish your building project, so that you can move forward. Does that sound acceptable?"

"Why, yes," Paul said. "That's more than acceptable. It's very generous, in fact. I'm flabbergasted, really."

"It's quite all right," Hans said. "There are some conditions, of course."

"Oh, of course," Paul said. "We can have the attorneys draw up the agreement, and work out the payment plan. I assure you that I will be prompt with my payments. Why, when I get that building finished--"

"I am not interested in the payment plan," Hans said. "I have other conditions."

"Oh?"

"First, I want to be your chief financial officer. If I am lending you money, I want to be able to see where it is being spent. I have a background in financial matters, and I can help you get your company back on the right track. You need discipline, Mr. Morley, and I can give you that."

"But I already have a financial man. His name's Peabody, and he's on top of the money situation. The man's a crackerjack--"

"He will have to find other employment," Hans said, firmly. "If you want my money, you must put me in charge of your books. That is not negotiable."

Paul hesitated. Peabody had been with the company for many years, and he hated to let him go. The chance to get all that cash, though, was too tempting.

"All right," he said. "It's a deal. I'll see if I can find a job for Peabody somewhere else, maybe with one of my customers. Is that it?"

"No. There is something else." The other man put down his drink and leaned forward, peering intently at Paul. "What are your feelings about this country?"

"This country? What do you mean?"

"Do you think it will survive this rough economic time we are going through?"

"Oh, of course," Paul said. "I think we basically have the right idea, and we'll come out all right. That is, if that old socialist in the White House doesn't destroy everything. If they'd leave it to the businesspeople, we'd have things humming again in no time. It's all these roadblocks they put up that cause the problems."

"Yes," Hans said. "I believe Roosevelt is part of the problem. The man is more than a socialist, he's a communist, don't you agree? I mean, I've heard he has Jewish blood in him, and you know more than half of the Bolsheviks running Russia are Jews. If we let those people run things, they'll turn the whole world communist."

"Maybe so," Paul said. "But I wouldn't compare us to Russia. I think our people have enough sense not to fall for that communist malarkey."

"Bah," Hans said, waving his hand in disgust. "You have too much faith in the people of this mongrel nation. They have come from every corner of the world, and they bring all their problems with them. They get here and start breeding with others of the refuse of nations, and they create a mongrel breed that threatens to pollute the European races. There are people who are born to run things, Mr. Morley, and others who only feed at the trough without giving back, and it has been that way for thousands of years. Most of the problems in this modern world come from the overthrow of the old ways, the supplanting of the pure races with the impure ones, and the degeneration of culture, religion, politics, and economics that comes from it."

He was leaning forward in his chair, as if he could barely keep from leaping out of it. The veins in his neck were bulging and there were flecks of white foam at the corners of his mouth.

Hans pulled out a white handkerchief and wiped his brow with it. He paused to get control of himself, then continued in a quieter voice. "You seem a reasonable man. I think you believe, as I and some others believe, that there needs to be some change, some reversal of the trend of modern life before it destroys us. That's why in return for my lending you some money I want your assistance in some activities."

"What type of activities?" Paul said.

"I belong to an organization that is standing firm against the threat of communism, socialism, the degeneration of culture due to racial impurity," Hans said. "You are aware of the situation in Europe? To be specific, in Germany?"

"Well, I don't pay too much attention to politics, but this fellow Hitler seems to be stirring up a lot of trouble."

"He is a beacon of light in the modern world!" Hans said. "He is fighting against the forces that would seek to destroy us. He is a great man, a champion of the Aryan way of life."

"Well I suppose so, but what does that have to do with me?"

"I need your help. My organization needs someone to act as a figurehead. We are supporters of Adolf Hitler and of Germany, and we want to get our message out. We need to put out a newspaper, some flyers promoting our rallies, some advertising materials. In other words, we need a lot of printing."

"I still don't understand what that has to do with me."

Hans looked at him as if he were a very stupid man, who could not comprehend the obvious. "You are in the paper industry. You sell to printing companies. I need your help in getting printers to work with us."

"I'm sure they will be happy to do business with you, Mr. Guenther. You won't need my help, as long as you can pay for their services."

"You are wrong," the other man said. "We have already approached them, and they do not want to do business with us. It seems we are too controversial. There is a lot of anti-German sentiment in this country, Mr. Morley, and some businesses are afraid of our organization. We need someone to act as a sort of go-between, someone who is an American by birth, whose loyalty cannot be questioned.

"We need a man who is good looking," he continued, "and can speak well, who will be a leader and a good front man. You fit that bill, Mr. Morley."

"Me? No, I'm not your man, Mr. Guenther. For one thing, I'm a child of immigrants myself. My family hasn't been in this country for five or six generations, like some others," he pointed to the window, through which they could hear the sounds of the orchestra and the guests chatting. "My mother was born in Ireland. We're new arrivals, compared to the people out there. You need one of them."

"There is no one out there who will do it," Hans said. "Don't you understand that? These people are not going to put themselves at risk, Mr. Morley. They do not operate that way. They prefer to be behind the scenes, conducting their affairs in privacy. They keep the machinery well oiled, and they make sure everything is running smoothly, but they don't ever get out in front. No, I need someone who is not quite of the ruling class, like yourself, a sort provisional member, who is convincing enough to play this role."

"You want me to lead your organization?"

"Precisely. Of course, you would be a leader in name only. I would make all the decisions, but you would be the person carrying them out. I would write the speeches; anything you say in public would come from me. Is it a deal?"

Paul stood up. "I thank you for meeting with me, Mr. Guenther, but there's no deal. I'm not your man. I won't be a party to this kind of scheme. I'm not a puppet, and I'm not interested in spouting slogans to promote that man Hitler, who from what I've heard is crazier than Roosevelt. I'll be seeing you."

He started to walk away, but Hans grabbed his arm.

"I would think carefully about what you're saying, Mr. Morley," he said, menace in his voice. "If you act rashly you'll be writing a death warrant for your company. You should think about all you stand to lose before you walk out of this room."

"I've thought about it," Paul said. "I'm not doing what you want."

"Okay," Hans said, relaxing his grip. "I will let you go. Also, I will wait till the end of the evening to hear your decision. I don't want you to make a decision that's too quick, something you'll regret later. Think about it, and let me know at the end of the night. Goodbye, Mr. Morley."

"Goodbye," Paul said. He strode out of the library with one thought in his mind: how to find Trudy as quickly as possible.

He found her in the garden, which was on a little terrace hidden away from the dance band and all the noise and activity of the party. She was fingering the petals of a pink rose growing by the side of a stone path. She turned to see him striding up the path toward her, and she smiled.

He had thought he would say something witty, but instead he simply reached out and touched her face with his hand. He touched it softly, lightly, just brushing his fingertips across her cheek. Her skin felt like velvet. She closed her eyes and tilted her head toward him, and he felt the flush of excitement in her cheek. He trembled with suppressed excitement. He did not know what was going to happen next, and he felt reckless and free. He had never done this with a woman before; and the fact that Lucy was somewhere on the grounds made it even more dangerously thrilling.

Then it happened. She brushed his hand aside, leaned into him, and kissed him full on the lips. Her lips were captivating, tender, vulnerable, thrilling, all at once. She put her arms around him and pulled him closer, till he felt her breasts against his shirt, her hips pressing against his pelvis. She enveloped him in her essence, her smell of cloves and roses filling the air and making his head spin. He cupped one hand on the small of her back, the other roamed among her silken hair, and he felt a charge like a thunderbolt running up and down his spine. His ran his fingertips down her neck, across her shoulder blade, and down her arm. She quivered with excitement, and he felt himself falling into a deep void, like someone who has dived off a cliff. A voice was telling him this was wrong, but he ignored it. The dance band was playing "Body And Soul," and he let the emotion carry him to new heights, as if they were dancing to a forbidden melody. He could not stop kissing her, and as she moaned softly it shattered the spell and he finally came to his senses and with a reflexive energy he broke away from her.

"I, I'm sorry," he said. "I should not have done that. I have to go, I have to, uh, I should go now."

He turned, but she grabbed his wrist and said, "Don't."

He almost kissed her again, but somehow he stopped himself. He left, hurrying up the garden path back to the party. He paused to collect himself, waiting till his heart stopped pounding in his chest, mopping the perspiration off his brow with a handkerchief, looking at his reflection in a garden pool to make sure there was no lipstick on him. He finally found Lucy and was the dutiful husband for the rest of the evening. He saw Trudy once, standing at the edge of the path that led down to the river, and she was looking straight at him. He quickly looked away and then started a conversation with a friend of Basil's. When he looked back, she was gone.

He could not get her out of his mind, however. The feel of her lips was permanently imprinted on his brain, her perfume was in his nostrils. Everything else about the evening now seemed pale and insubstantial. Only the few moments with her seemed real.

He socialized as though nothing had changed, laughed at people's jokes and even danced a few numbers with Lucy. It was like moving about in a dream, with a strange unreality to all the shapes and people moving in and out of his field of vision.

When it was time to go, he told Lucy there was someone he had to say goodbye to, and he slipped away and found Hans in the library, drinking his scotch and staring into the fire.

Hans looked up at him, and the ghost of a smile played on his lips. "So? Have you made a decision, Mr. Morley?" he said.

Paul looked at him. "I'll do it," he said. Then he walked out of the room.

CHAPTER SEVEN

May, 1938

"Rosie!" the boy Lukas yelled. "Come down now, you are too far up in the tree!"

"Stop being such a wet blanket," Rosie shouted. "I like it up here, and I'm not coming down!"

"But if you fall, you'll get killed!"

She was in her special place, at the top of the oak tree in the backyard of her house, 40 feet in the air, so high that she could see all the way to the massive Sears & Roebuck building 20 miles away, and on clear days, if she turned her head just the right way she could even see the City Hall tower further south. Rosie loved climbing up here and sitting in a crook of the tree and thinking. It was where she could try to make sense of things, make them all right in her head.

"Rosie! Come down or I am going to go in and tell your mother! This is dangerous!"

"If you're so worried, why don't you climb up here and save me?"

"I would, only I don't want to get my uniform dirty. I have to go to a meeting later, and I must keep it clean."

"That's a stupid excuse. It's just a silly uniform anyway, and you go to silly meetings in it, so who cares if it gets dirty? You're just too scared. Too scared to climb up here!"

She giggled as she heard him fuming far below her. "Scared" was a word that always got boys to do what you wanted them to do. They couldn't afford to show any weakness in front of girls, she knew that.

The branches below her started to shake, and she heard his shoes scraping on the bark of the tree as he climbed. He slipped once, shouted an angry curse, and then continued climbing. As he got closer, she could hear him panting.

Finally his head appeared through the branches, his blonde hair tousled and his face pink with exertion. With a grunt, he pulled himself up to a sitting position on a branch just below her. She was sitting in just such a way that he could see up her pinafore, and she let him take a look before she closed her legs.

"You are the most frustrating girl," he said, still out of breath. "Look at this, I've torn the sleeve of my uniform." He held out his arm, and the gray sleeve of his military style uniform was hanging loosely. "Why do you insist on being so difficult?"

"This is my tree," she said. "I climb up here when I need some peace. What's wrong with that?"

"Girls don't climb trees," he said. "It's not right. You are the strangest girl I ever saw."

"Oh? What should I be doing? Making schnitzels like the girls in your stupid youth group do? I don't do things like that, I never have."

"Girls in Germany don't climb trees."

"We're not in Germany. This is America, Lukas, in case you didn't realize it. And you were born here, so you're an American. I don't know what's so special about Germany, anyway. I like it here."

He stared at her with his shockingly blue eyes, eyes that she could get lost in so easily, before he finally answered.

"My father says Germany is the greatest place in the world. He said the country is so beautiful, especially in Bavaria. And the people, they're the purest, most handsome people in the world. He says the men are all strong and blonde, and the women are like goddesses. He says--"

"I know what he says, I've heard all this before," Rosie said. "I've heard him droning on to my father about it for hours. He drives me crazy with all that talk. Why doesn't he just take you all back to Germany then?"

"Some day," Lukas said, a faraway look coming into his eyes. "When we win back the lands that are ours. When the Fuhrer helps us to regain our rightful place in the world."

Rosie didn't like Lukas' father. He was a short man named Hans with a wire brush of a mustache, a clipped haircut and a way of speaking that made you think he had no doubt that he was right all the time. He spoke to Rosie like she was a three year old, and when she answered him in what her mother called her smart aleck voice, his eyes widened and he looked like he wanted to take her over his knee and give her a good spanking. He had been coming around to their house for a couple of years now. Her father introduced him as a business associate, and they often had hushed conferences in the study or on the front porch. Rosie's mother didn't seem to like him either, but she kept her mouth shut, seeming to not want to cause trouble.

But that wasn't the only reason Rosie didn't like him. She could pinpoint the time when her father and mother's problems started, the coldness that came between them, and it was when Lukas' father started coming around. Or, to be more precise, when his father and mother came around.

The mother was a tall, aristocratic woman with the carriage of a ballet dancer and the face of an empress. She had blonde hair braided in a bun, and she had cheekbones that seemed chiseled by a sculptor. She had an aura of elegance about her, and Rosie could see the change in her father's face when she was around.

She knew things, Rosie did. She sensed them. She knew that her father liked Lukas' mother, even before she found them kissing in the grape arbor one evening. It was an evening a month ago in April and her father and mother were hosting one of their dinner parties. It was a dreadfully boring affair, as they all were, and Rosie could not wait to get away from it. After dinner the guests congregated in the living room, where they'd rolled back the rugs and danced to the music from the Victrola. As the sky darkened outside Rosie got a strange feeling in the pit of her stomach, and she realized her father was missing, along with Lukas' mother. She knew that feeling; it meant she was going to see something, and a picture flashed in her mind of the grape arbor. She snuck out the back door and down the winding path that led to it.

Before she ever got there she heard them: the low, intimate tone in their voices, the softness that seemed like a slap in the face.

They were standing at the far end of the long tunnel-like trellis that was covered in grape vines, and they were silhouetted against the light of the setting sun behind them. Rosie crouched at one end, unable to make out their words but understanding nonetheless what they were saying. They were in each other's arms, and Rose saw the woman with her head on her father's shoulder.

She could have crept closer and gotten a better look, but she felt evil wafting toward her like the smell of something rotten, and she did not want to get close to it.

She turned and went back to the house, and she waited at the top of the stairs and listened to the bright, sparkling voices till she could make out that her father and the woman had returned. They laughed and joked with the other people and nothing seemed to be amiss.

Rose knew, though, that things were upside down now, and might never get straight again.

The world was going crazy, it seemed. The adults played golf and laughed and went to parties, and meanwhile the news on the radio and in the newspapers was of approaching war. Lukas's father was the leader of a local German American organization, and he gave speeches about things like racial purity and the glory of Germany. There was a young people's organization, called Pure Youth, and they wore uniforms and did military drills at a summer camp in Sellersville PA.

"Rosie I insist, climb down this moment!" Lukas said. He was trying to be stern, but he was holding on to a branch for dear life, clearly more worried about falling out of the tree than anything else.

"What is it your father does, besides making speeches and running rallies?" Rose said, ignoring his command.

"I don't know for sure," Lukas said. "He's an investor, I think. He invested in your father's company. They're partners now. Now our families are linked. It is good, don't you think?"

"Maybe." She didn't like Lukas's parents, and she didn't like the way he was so obsessed with Germany, but she had to admit he was a handsome boy. He had that smooth translucent skin and corn silk blonde hair, and those eyes that seemed like the blue sky after you came out of a long tunnel.

"Why do you come up here?" Lukas said. "There's no need for this."

"Because it's peaceful. I can think up here. And I like looking out at the world. You can see for miles up here. I like to think about strange things. Do you think there's a God?"

"What a silly question. Of course there is. He's looking out for all of us. Holding us in His hand, as my father says."

"You think he gets involved in our lives like that?"

"Yes I do. He loves us all, and cares about every part of our lives. He knows what is right and just, and he doesn't want to see us pollute our blood with racial mixing."

"Oh, that's hogwash. I can't believe a God would care about that racial nonsense. Besides, all people are equal."

Lukas' eyes widened. "No they're not. Not at all. There are the Aryan races and then the lower ones. They must not be mixed. Our race is the best, and God put us here to rule over the others. Don't you understand that?"

"No, I don't," she said. "It sounds like so much bullshit to me."

"Lucy!" Lukas said. "You should watch your language."

"I can say what I want up here. And you're talking a bunch of horse manure."

"No I am not," he said, his face clouding over. "There is going to be a war. My father has assured me of that. The European countries do not want to have a strong German nation, so they want to crush us. We must be prepared! We must be strong, and we will win."

"War is stupid," Rosie said. "People killing each other to solve their quarrels. There must be a better way than that."

"There is no better way, because the world is unjust and sinful, and people will lie and cheat to get their way. There is a right order to things, and sometimes war is needed to put things back to their right order."

Rose wondered if Lukas knew what his mother and her father were doing. She thought about telling him, but the opaqueness in his innocent blue eyes put her off. He probably wouldn't believe me, she thought. It would be like telling him the sun was blue.

"I don't want to talk about this anymore," she said. "We should climb down now. Come on!"

She started to shimmy down the tree trunk, and she had to climb past Lukas to get down. Somehow she maneuvered her body past him, and as she did she slipped on a branch and fell into him.

He grabbed onto a branch with one hand and put the other arm around her waist.

"Careful!" he said. "You'll fall."

He was staring at her with those astonishing blue eyes, and his lips were open in horror, and on an impulse she wrapped her arms around him and kissed him full on the lips. His lips tasted sweet and fresh, and she felt a wave of excitement take shape inside her, and her breath came hot and her heart pounded in her chest. It was just a moment, an instant, really, but it seemed like Time stopped.

Then, she pushed away from him, looked at those blue eyes again, his mouth agape, and she scrambled down the tree trunk, grabbing ahold of all the familiar branches, sticking her feet in all the right places, until she was at the bottom, where she ran away laughing with the joy of being alive.

CHAPTER EIGHT

August 31, 1939

Martin had to stop to catch his breath halfway up the steps to the auditorium. This struggle to breathe was happening more these days. He knew he should go to the doctor about it, but he didn't think it would do much good. I'm 79 years old, he told himself; I'm like an old horse that ought to be put out to pasture. His vision was getting worse too, and on evenings like tonight, after a long day of poring over legal documents, his sight was blurry and indistinct. He didn't want to worry Rose, so he rarely spoke about it, but he had a feeling that the number of his days was diminishing.

Normally he would have been riding the subway home at this hour, but he'd told Rose he had some business tonight. Actually, it had nothing to do with business; he wanted to see for himself what was going on at these rallies that Paul was involved in. They were put on by something called the German American Fraternal Society, and Paul insisted it was simply a harmless cultural organization when Martin had gone to see him about it.

He'd sat at Paul's big desk in his office with the windows that overlooked the river and the new building Paul was putting up at his paper company. Paul beamed with pride as he pointed out the big cranes and the hordes of construction workers in their hard hats like so many worker bees far below. "We'll be the largest paper company on the East Coast when I get finished," he'd said. "That is, of course, if that damned fool Roosevelt doesn't drive us out of business with his policies."

Paul was a dyed in the wool Republican now, and he railed against Roosevelt and the Democrats constantly. Lately, however, it seemed that it involved more than the complaints of a businessman who disagreed with his government's economic policy. A note of anger and paranoia and something else, a racial supremacism, had crept into his conversation.

When Martin questioned him about it, though, he rebuffed it with a laugh. "I'm just facing facts, old boy. Our society is degenerating, going through a process of mongrelization. All these communists and their nonsensical talk about equality, that's the root of the problem. People are not equal, Martin, some of us are different than others. We should support the people like the Germans who are from the same bloodlines as us."

"You're getting all this from that man Guenther, right?" Martin said. "That little Prussian drill sergeant with the beautiful wife. From what I've seen of him, he's trouble. I'd stay away from him, if I were you."

"You've got the wrong idea about him, old boy," Paul said. "He's a voice of sanity in this crazy world. He's telling us what's important, the things we should value. We're in such a rush to help all these freeloaders, these parasites who don't give anything back, that we don't realize what we're losing."

"That's not what I've heard," Martin said. "Your friend Guenther is a supporter of that mad German Hitler. Don't you read the newspapers? Why, last November they burned and looted synagogues, destroyed shops, killed people just for being Jewish. That man is a powder keg, Paul, and anyone who gets mixed up with him will have trouble. And, by the way, I know there are people in the police department who are keeping an eye on Guenther. There's talk of war with Germany, you know that. It's not a good idea to get mixed up with a fellow like him, who's making these inflammatory speeches."

"Not to worry," Paul said. "Really, he's not saying anything that millions of people aren't thinking. He's a voice of reason, I guarantee you. Tell you what: why don't you come to one of the rallies we hold at the Athenaeum on Walnut Street. We usually get a few thousand people, and it's a whale of an evening -- more fun than listening to "Fibber McGee And Molly" on the radio. You'll see for yourself that Hans Guenther is not a troublemaker. He's just a man who's trying to promote friendship between two great nations."

The whole business was so troubling to Martin that he couldn't bring himself to actually go to one of the rallies for quite a while. He put it out of his mind for months, but finally, he figured he'd better see what was going on, especially since he kept getting signals from his contacts in the criminal justice system that Paul was being watched.

So, Martin was here, making his way into the auditorium, where there was a German brass band playing on a stage draped with German and American flags. The music from the tubas and trombones throbbed and there was a festive atmosphere everywhere. There were pictures on the stage of various people, both living and dead, including two of Adolf Hitler smiling and looking quite benign.

"Martin Lancaster, is that you?"

Martin turned to see a big Irish policeman he knew as Mick O'Reilly, a beefy man with a penchant for whiskey and jokes. "How are you, Mick? I see they have you on duty tonight."

"Yes, and a pity it is, too," O'Reilly said. "I'm missing my weekly poker game because of it. I'd rather be sitting at a table with a handful of cards and a good stiff whiskey at me side than to be stuck here listening to these boring speeches. And what are you doing here, counselor? I didn't think you were involved in this German American business."

"I'm just here to see my son-in-law, Paul Morley," Martin said. "He's one of the speakers, and he invited me to come."

O'Reilly's florid face colored deeper red, and he said, "I know he's mixed up in it, and it's a shameful thing, if you ask me, a son of Irish immigrants like himself making speeches about superior races and all that. It's what we came over here to get away from. I knew him a bit growing up and I was always proud of the lad, making his way to the top of the heap the way he did. Now, I don't know what's come over him, with all that palaver about racial purity."

"Well, that's why I'm here," Martin said, "to judge for myself whether he's gone off the deep end. I'll monitor the situation, Mick, don't you worry."

"You do that, counselor," O'Reilly said. "However, I'd be careful, if I was you, with this crowd of mischief makers. I've worked these rallies before, and there's a good number of these fellows who have short fuses. They get all fired up by the end of the night, and they're looking for someone to pop in the mouth. Many's the night I've had to knock their heads together or even throw a couple of them in the back of a paddy wagon and let them cool their heels in a cell for a few hours. You watch yourself, counselor."

"Don't worry," Martin said. "I'm too old for fighting, and I avoid conflict at all costs."

He moved off and found a seat in front of the stage, where he'd be able to see clearly. The band was still playing its jaunty music and the atmosphere was festive, but when the hall had finished filling up with people, all of a sudden the band came to a stop, and the musicians packed up their instruments and left. A curtain opened at the back of the stage and Paul strode out, looking handsome in a navy blue suit, white shirt and red tie, his hair combed back neatly and his white teeth gleaming. He looked the picture of vitality and strength.

"Good evening!" he said. "We have a wonderful night in store for you, so let's get started."

Martin could see that Paul enjoyed being in the limelight. He seemed to bask in the glow of the lights, and he had a performer's delight in the crowd's attention. He struck poses, gripping the podium with both hands, holding one hand aloft and jabbing the air with his index finger to make a point, wagging his head with scorn after he made a reference to the hated Franklin Roosevelt, sighing with regret over some nostalgic word picture he painted of the better days that America had enjoyed "before the socialist crowd got in the White House". It was theater, and Martin could see that Paul was putting on a show. He wasn't so sure that Paul believed everything he was saying, but he clearly enjoyed saying it in front of this crowd, which applauded him with boisterous enthusiasm.

It was a different matter when Hans Guenther spoke, though. The little man strode briskly out to the podium and began immediately to launch into a shrill harangue against "Jews, Jew lovers, and all who would pollute the greatness of the Northern European races". He baited the crowd, throwing out one inflammatory slogan after another, pulling the applause from them like a lion tamer making his charges jump through hoops. "Have you had enough?" he would say, and the crowd would roar, "Yes!" with one voice.

Martin was disturbed by this spectacle, and even with his poor eyes he could see that the little man looked dangerous, his eyes blazing and the veins in his neck bulging, little gobs of spittle flying out of his mouth with every shouted epithet.

The air in the room seemed supercharged, and Martin felt sweat break out on his forehead. There was an ugliness here you could feel; it was like a dark presence hovering behind Guenther, at the edges of Martin's vision. The people around Martin in the audience were moving with an edgy energy, leaping up from their seats, pumping their fists in the air, their teeth bared, their eyes glittering with hate.

Martin had seen enough. He got up from his seat, pushed his way past the people in the front row, and then headed down the center aisle toward the back.

The crowd was becoming louder and more agitated by the minute, and Martin hoped he could get out before anything bad happened. He could see massive oak doors at the back, and there were a few policemen there, plus some of the gray-shirted members of Guenther's paramilitary force, their arms crossed in front of their chests and their faces looking stern.

Martin was halfway there, when all of a sudden the oak doors opened and a crowd of young men swarmed in. Some of them carried signs with slogans, and Martin could make out Jewish stars on them. They began chanting "Down With Hitler," and "Nazis Out Of America" and they were clearly trying to drown out the sound of Guenther's voice.

The gray-shirted guards didn't waste any time; they waded into the crowd of demonstrators and started swinging their fists, and some of them used blackjacks. They must have been expecting this; it didn't seem to faze them at all. The demonstrators fought back, swinging their placards like weapons, shouting all the while.

This was exactly the kind of trouble Martin had been worried about, and he looked around to see if there were any other exits. By this time the crowd had noticed the disturbance in the back of the hall, and hordes of them came stampeding up the aisle to get into the fight. Martin was knocked backward by the crowd, and he ended up on the floor, with people scrambling over him to get to the melee. I'm done for now, he thought. I'll get trampled by this mob before I can get up.

All of a sudden there were two hands under his arms, and someone lifted him up from behind. He could not see in the pandemonium, but the next thing he knew he was being lifted up and thrown over someone's shoulder. He bounced around through the crowd, bumping into people on all sides, and he heard the gruff Irish accent of Mick O'Reilly telling people to make way.

After running the gauntlet of people at the back of the hall Martin found himself being deposited in a chair in a small coatroom, where O'Reilly looked at him with concern and said, "Are ye all right, counselor?"

"I'm fine," Martin said. "Thank you for saving me. I could have been squashed like a bug out there."

"'Twas nothing," O'Reilly said. "But now, if you'll excuse me, I have an appointment to knock some heads together. Just stay here, counselor, 'tis a dangerous lot of them, and you don't want to get hurt."

"It's hard to believe we've come to settling our differences with fists," Martin said.

"Aye, but that's what happens when you stir up trouble like that blasted Guenther fellow," O'Reilly said. "It doesn't bode well for the situation in Europe, let me tell you."

"No, it doesn't," Martin said. "Nor, for my son-in-law, I'm afraid."

CHAPTER NINE

August 31, 1939

Edith could hear the raised voices in the back of the store, and she knew that Simon was having an argument with his nephew Avram once again. The boy was a headstrong 19 year old, and lately he had been clashing more and more with his uncle. It was mostly about the world situation, she knew. Simon was on a knife edge all the time about his relatives in Germany, especially since the Kristallnacht episode last year, when the Nazis had evicted thousands of Jews from their homes and businesses, in an orgy of burning, looting, and violence that was truly barbaric. She knew that Simon could not sleep at night for worrying about his relatives, and some had disappeared in the aftermath of the violence, leaving Simon to wonder if they had been killed or shipped off to concentration camps.

The boy Avram had become increasingly angry and confrontational through all of this. He bridled at his uncle's attempts to control him, and he was running with a crowd of other young Jewish boys who seemed just as angry. He went to secret meetings with them, and he came home spouting angry slogans and calls for violence against the government because it was ignoring the plight of the Jews in Europe.

Edith worried that the boy would do something rash, and she tried to intervene when she could, attempting to be a calming presence, a mediator between Simon and the boy. Now, though, judging from the volume of their voices, things seemed to be coming to a head.

There were no customers to wait on so she made her way to the back to see if she could help Simon talk some reason to his nephew. She went down the long, narrow room that formed the store and opened the door that led to the cramped back room that opened on an alley in the back where the deliverymen dropped off the boxes of fruit, vegetables and other items Simon sold.

"But why must you do this?" Simon was saying, anguish in his voice. Edith noticed that he had more lines in his face than when she had first come to work for him. The worry was aging him. "You are asking for trouble, going to this rally."

"Why am I doing it?" Avram said. "You must be joking, uncle. Have you seen this?" He held up a poster he had obviously torn down from a telephone pole, and it had a picture of a German flag on it. "Come and hear the truth!" it said in big block letters. "There is no time to lose! Stop the lies about Germany! Support the fight to keep America pure!" It had a cartoon figure of Franklin Roosevelt with a long nose and a black top hat, shaking the hand of Joseph Stalin.

Avram threw the poster on the floor and spat on it. "This is why I have to go! We must fight this kind of nonsense. We must fight back, or this country will be like Germany."

Simon shook his head. "Listen to yourself. Fighting is not the answer. If you go to that rally I am worried that you will get hurt. My sister will never forgive me if something happens to you."

"Your sister!" Avram sneered. "You don't even know if she's alive. She could be in a Nazi concentration camp at this very moment, but the world doesn't care. We must do something, or we will all be wiped out!"

His face was flushed, and he was clenching his fists as if he wanted to fight. He is scared, Edith saw. She reached out and touched him on the arm, but he brushed her off. "Get away," he snarled. "This is not your fight, it is mine."

"Fighting will not solve this," Edith said. "I think you should listen to your uncle. He is concerned for your well being."

"Bah!" the boy said. "He is afraid, like all the rest of them. We will never be free until we have the courage to fight our oppressors."

"There are other things you can do," Simon said. "We have Jewish organizations that are trying to get Roosevelt to recognize the problem."

"He will do nothing," the boy said. "Don't you understand that?" He picked up the poster from the floor and waved it in his uncle's face. "And this is why! We are not welcome here, uncle."

Simon shook his head. "I don't believe that. I came here fifteen years ago with nothing, and I had to borrow money just to set up a little pushcart selling vegetables. Now look -- I have my own store! People here stretched out their arms to me, helped me. It is different here. You must have faith, Avram. We have a home here, you'll understand that some day. For now, however--"

"For now I am done listening to all your old man talk," Avram said. He threw the poster on the floor and ran out the back door, pushing Simon aside so violently that he toppled against a crate of apples, scattering them to the floor.

Edith helped him to his feet, and she saw that there were tears in his eyes. "He will be all right," she said. "He's just a boy, and they act rashly sometimes."

"Yes, but he's my responsibility!" Simon said, his voice choking with emotion. "I cannot have someone else in my family be in danger, Edith. It is too much, too much."

She put her arms around him and tried to comfort him. He felt thinner, his clothes hanging on him loosely. She knew he had not been eating enough, could not bring himself to eat much lately.

"You must take care of yourself," she said, stroking his hair. "I am worried about you. It will all work out, believe me."

"I cannot let any harm come to him," Simon said. "I have no control over what happens in Germany, but I must look after whatever family I have here. I know what I have to do." He straightened up and pulled his coat around him as if he had made his mind up.

"What do you mean?" she said. "What are you going to do?"

"I am going to go to that rally tonight."

* *

Simon wanted to go alone, but Edith insisted that she accompany him to the rally. "I will not let you go by yourself," she said. "You're older than me, and I don't want anything bad to happen to you. I won't lose you, Simon."

He seemed touched by her words, but she meant them. She wasn't going to let her natural English reserve hold her back any longer. There was no point in beating around the bush anymore; she had determined to say what was on her mind, and to tell the people in her life what they meant to her. She had not done that with James, and it always gnawed at her.

The rally was in an old auditorium called the Athenaeum, and it had been used twenty years ago for vaudeville shows. Now it was more often used for lectures and readings, and rallies like this. They passed by men in uniforms of gray shirts and black pants, wearing shiny black knee boots and black belts with large brass buckles on them. They wore short-billed black hats and many of them had mustaches. They looked vaguely military, and they stood with their arms crossed and watched the crowd filing in to the hall.

Inside there was a German brass band playing on the stage, and there were German and American flags, along with pictures of Adolf Hitler, and famous Germans from American history, such as Von Steuben, the Prussian officer who had helped during the American Revolution.

There were perhaps five hundred people here, Edith estimated, but she could not see Avram in the crowd. Simon made his way down the center aisle and found seats for Edith and himself about ten rows from the stage. There was a festive air because of the brassy music from the band, but that didn't take away the feeling of foreboding Edith had. There was a look of anger on many of the faces in the crowd, a sneering curl of the lip, a hint that there was an evil, pent up energy wanting to get out. Simon kept swiveling his head in wonder, his eyes wide, like he could not believe this was happening in the city he thought he knew. He was very quiet, but Edith knew it was because he was very worried.

Then the band stopped abruptly, and the musicians began to put away their instruments. A man strode out to the podium and Edith felt a chill run down her spine. She recognized him from four years ago, when James had died. He was James's son from his first marriage, a man named Paul Morley. He was beaming like a politician, clearly very happy to be on stage. He greeted the crowd and began to tell them what a great evening was in store, and he launched into a speech about the current political situation, sprinkled with a lot of lines that got applause. What bothered Edith was the casual way he used slogans and jokes that belittled Jews and other ethnic groups. Does he not realize that he's the son of an Irishman who experienced prejudice?

James had not talked much of his past, but when he did he said that he was "barefoot and hungry" his whole childhood and that he'd seen horrible injustice at the hands of the British soldiers. "It's a great country we're in, isn't it, my girl?" he'd say, sweeping his hand around like a grandee. "Why, there's opportunity here for every man, no matter where he comes from." It was a mystery to Edith how his son could be standing up there using words to divide people into the old classifications, keeping them forever in their boxes.

But he was nothing compared to what came later. After a parade of other speakers, various "experts" on the world situation, interspersed with some musical interludes when singers would come up and sing patriotic songs, Paul Morley introduced a man he said was "a patriot, a friend of our two great countries, and a man with the courage to say what we need to hear about the world's problems and what to do about them."

A short, compact man strode briskly out to the podium, amid wild applause and cheering. He had a russet mustache and hair that stood up stiffly from his head. He glared at the audience from steel blue eyes. He began calmly, in a measured tone, making his points one by one, telling the rapt audience about the injustices Germany had suffered at the hands of the European victors in the last war, how after many years of suffering they had found a savior in Adolf Hitler, a man who had the strength of character to bring them out of the wilderness and back into their rightful place among the countries of the world. As he went on his voice got louder and more shrill, and he started to jab his finger in the air to make his points. Simon fidgeted in his seat, and Edith could tell he was getting more upset by the things this man was saying. The man was now talking in slogans, shouting things like "The Jew Roosevelt" and "No More Race Mixing," and the veins in his neck were prominent and his eyes were bulging. The crowd looked at him with rapt attention, many of them mouthing the slogans as he said them, and they were becoming increasingly agitated.

Edith felt fear clutch at her, when she realized that everyone sitting around them was shouting, some of them standing up in their seats, and they looked eager for a fight. She noticed that Simon was trembling, and she worried that he might have a heart attack, or that the strain on him would cause him to have a stroke.

"Simon, l want to leave," she said. "We need to go. Now." She took his hand and started to stand up, when all of a sudden there was a noise at the back of the hall. There were shouts, a noise like breaking glass, and a thudding sound like fists connecting with other bodies. Edith turned to see a mob of young men pouring through the doors at the back of the hall, and they were attacking the gray shirted men she had seen earlier. There were fists flying, curses, placards being swung like weapons, a gasp from the audience as they realized what was happening. Edith saw policemen wading into the crowd, their nightsticks flying, and there was blood already spraying like colored water. "Simon," she said, clutching his hand.

"Please. Let us find some way to get out of here. Maybe there is a side door."

They stood up, but then Simon saw something, and froze. "It is Avram!" he said. "I saw him back there."

"We cannot help him," Edith said. "Please, Simon. We must get out of here before someone pulls out a gun. There could be shooting. Let's go!"

She pulled at him, but he turned to her with tears in his eyes. "No! I cannot leave my nephew. I must go help him."

Edith tried to pull him away, but he brushed her off and then disappeared into the crowd. "Simon, don't leave!" she shouted, reaching for his hand, but he was gone.

She was horrified, lost in a sea of hate, and she made her way through the swirling bodies and tried to find a safe haven, somewhere away from the madness all around her. There were shouts of fear, anger, bewilderment coming from every direction, and she did not know where to go. Finally she somehow made her way to the stage, and she climbed up the half a dozen steps to the top of it. She found herself standing just a few feet away from the hateful little man who had incited the crowd, and he was looking out at the pandemonium and smiling.

"You odious man," she said, going over and grabbing him by the sleeve. "See what you started. You are to blame for this."

He pulled his arm away and looked at her coldly. "It is only a symptom of the times," he said. "It will get worse before it gets better."

"I would slap you, except I don't believe in violence," Edith said. "But you should be ashamed to call yourself a human being."

"I am not ashamed," he said. "Not at all. But I must go. There are enemies out there who would like to kill me, and I must live to fight another day."

And then he slipped through the curtain at the back of the stage and was gone.

CHAPTER TEN

September 1, 1939

The sun was streaming through the window of the Ritz Carlton, and Paul woke up with a smile on his face. It was one of those days where you could face anything, he decided, take on any task and assert your will.

This is the day. I'm going to tell Lucy I'm leaving her today. No time like the present, and I'll just go ahead and do it.

It was time. Great things were happening in his life, and he needed to make a break with Lucy, to move forward the way his heart was telling him to.

After all, he had just had one of the best nights of his life last night. He had been on stage as master of ceremonies at a rally that had a great crowd of people in attendance, all of them watching and listening intently to his every word. He had been in command, with all those upturned faces gazing at him, and he felt powerful. Sure, there had been some trouble at the end, a disturbance with some hooligans who'd tried to break up the rally, but that was to be expected. There were people who just didn't like Hans Guenther's organization, and there had been violence several times lately.

It didn't matter. It would all turn out right, he was sure of that. This talk of war with Germany was silly; Guenther told him it would never happen. It would all blow over, and things would be just a rosy as before, even better when that fiend Roosevelt left office. The people would see the error of their ways, and people like Paul and Hans Guenther would be hailed for the true patriots they really were.

He reached next to him for Trudy, but there was nothing there in the bed. He smiled as he remembered last night with her. He had felt like a stallion, he had so much energy, and Trudy had urged him on repeatedly, whispering in German, driving him half mad with her cries and whispers, her mysterious elusiveness even in the most intimate of moments. She was never fully there, and Paul wanted her there, wanted to possess her in every way, to have every shred of her being, without secrets or mysteries.

Now she was gone, the same way she had left on other mornings. She had gotten up early, tiptoed around like a ghost, not disturbing the membrane of his fitful sleep, and she was gone.

No matter. He was too happy today, too energized, to let it bother him for long. He would eat a quick breakfast in the hotel restaurant, then drive to the office. Later, he would have his talk with Lucy.

He had told Lucy he was staying in town because of his duties at the political rally. It was true, of course, that he had finished with the rally very late, and that it would have been much too late to drive home, just like other rallies. The part he never mentioned was that Trudy slept next to him in the hotel bed.

He felt different, alive in a way he hadn't felt in years. It was exciting to be on a stage, and to have people looking at him in that special way that audiences have, hanging on his every word.

He was never the top speaker at these events. There was always someone else, some writer or businessman or politician who was the main event, followed by Guenther. Paul was there to warm up the audience, and he had gotten good at it. He threw out all the lines about the socialists in the government and how Stalin and the Bolsheviks wanted to rule the world, and how countries could go downhill fast if they let the races mix together -- all that stuff that Hans wrote for him. He had a polished delivery now, and he knew how to time his cadences and his movements so he got the greatest applause lines.

Last night had been the biggest rally yet, and there were thousands of men in attendance, some of them giving "Heil Hitler" salutes, and wearing uniforms. The police were in attendance too, and it was a good thing, because a local Jewish group showed up and started a tussle in the back of the great hall, and the police had to intervene with their truncheons and their fists.

It was all so much more exciting than the paper business, which continued to sputter along in the miserable economy, even with Paul's expensive new building and all the spanking new equipment he had bought.

Paul got dressed and came downstairs on the elevator to the restaurant, and the first thing he saw was a stack of newspapers in a bin by the entrance to the dining room, and they had a headline in block letters that said: "Germany Invades Poland!".

Paul gasped. Hans had told him that Germany would never cause a war, no matter how aggressive Hitler's speeches were, no matter how much he built up its army and navy. It's all just posturing, Hans said, a way to raise Germany's profile in the world. "Hitler doesn't want war," Hans claimed. "He doesn't want German citizens to be killed or maimed. He just wants Germany to have its rightful place in the world."

This newspaper headline couldn't be true, could it? Paul suddenly had no appetite for breakfast. He went to the front door and paid the valet to retrieve his yellow Packard with the black leather seats, and when the man brought the car around he got in and raced off to the office on Delaware Avenue.

He had to talk to Hans. Hans had been to Germany several times in the last few years. He had been to a dinner where Hitler spoke. He knew people in the government. He had told Paul there were no plans to start a war; it was all just lies spread by the European powers, who didn't want a strong Germany and were trying to contain it, to pen Germany up like a caged animal. Paul believed him. He had done what Hans asked, been the front man for Hans' political group, and he had enjoyed making the speeches and assuming an air of power and influence. He didn't really believe all of the things he was saying, but he was happy to get applause by saying them.

He didn't think any of it would come true. He had been in a war, back in 1918, and he knew how stupid and insane and brutal they could be. He did not believe that anyone would want that kind of insanity again. Surely, the people in power, the elites, would keep something like that from breaking out again.

He pulled in to his parking spot in front of the office, and he noticed clouds and rain squalls over the river, making his new building look gloomy and forlorn. It looked like a hulking pile of cement and bricks, ugly and squat.

He tried to cheer himself up. It will all work out. As soon as I get in to the office I'll call Hans; he's bound to have a good explanation for what's going on.

He took the elevator up to the third floor, got off and made his way back to his office. He greeted Gladys with a hearty "Good Morning", but she seemed disturbed about something.

"There's a few fellows here to see you," she said.

"At this time of the morning?" he said, looking around the waiting room.

"They're already in there," she said, pointing to the closed door of his office.

"Who are they?" he asked.

"I'm sorry, Mr. Morley, but they wouldn't say. They just said to send you in as soon as you got here. I tried to get rid of them, but they wouldn't take no for an answer."

Paul was annoyed at being forced to have an unscheduled meeting this early in the morning. He opened the door and strode in, covering his annoyance with a breezy air. "So, what do you fellows mean, darkening my door at this hour? I have a business to run, and this is highly irregular."

There were two men in dark suits sitting at his desk, and they had the world-weary, jaded look of detectives. They looked impatient, as if they had expected him to arrive earlier. One of them, a rawboned fellow who had a square chin and a brown fedora hat and was obviously the leader, said, "Sit down, Mr. Morley. We have a few things to talk about."

Paul sat down across from them, and he noticed that the other man, who wore a black fedora, had a newspaper in his lap with the headlines about Hitler's invasion of Poland across the front page.

"I'll get right to the point," the man in the brown fedora said. "What do you know about Hans Guenther?"

"Now see here," Paul said. "What do you mean, barging into my office and interrogating me this way? I don't have to answer your questions. Just who are you fellows, anyway?"

The men looked at each other and smiled, amused at his show of bravado.

"My name is Joe Murphy," the man in the brown hat said. "This is my partner Francis Latham." The other man nodded a perfunctory hello.

"We're from the Treasury Department," Murphy said. He reached in his pocket and pulled out a badge, as did Latham. They flashed the badges at Paul, then put them back in their coat pockets.

"Calm down, Mr. Morley," Murphy said. "Make yourself comfortable. We'll be here for awhile." He took his hat off, as did his partner Latham.

Paul suddenly felt very tired. "What do you want to know?" he asked. It seemed like all the air had gone out of the world, and he felt much older than he had when he woke up this morning.

"Guenther," Murphy said. "We want to know about Hans Guenther. He's an associate of yours, I understand. They tell me he even works here. That right, Morley?"

"He does the books for my company, if that's what you mean," Paul said. "He handles the finances."

Latham let out a guffaw. It was like the sound of a horse laughing. Murphy shot a glance at him, smiling.

"What's so funny?" Paul said.

"Oh, nothing," Murphy said, grinning. "It's just that I don't know if Hans Guenther is the fellow I'd want to be handling my money."

"What do you mean? He's a crackerjack man with money. I have complete trust in him."

"I see," Murphy said. "How long have you known him?"

"Oh, about four years now, I suppose."

"You do a lot of work for that organization of his, the German American Fraternal Society, right?"

"Yes."

"You believe in all that racial purity stuff?" Latham said. It was the first time he had spoken, and Paul saw that he had large teeth to go with his lantern jaw and his long nose.

"Well, I think there are differences between the races," Paul said. "I mean, some people are just born with more, don't you think? They're a cut above the rest. They're smarter, healthier, better in every way. A lot of our problems today come from people trying to pretend we're all equal. We're not equal; there are differences. We should just acknowledge that and stop all this socialist nonsense about equality. We won't get anywhere by diluting the purity of the races, I'll tell you that."

The two men looked at him like he was a curiosity, something you'd stare at in a sideshow at a carnival. Paul resented it immensely, and his color rose.

"You mark my words," he said. "No good will come of these policies that tyrant Roosevelt is putting into place. This country had better wake up and put the brakes on, or we're all going to be taken over by Joe Stalin and the boys in Moscow."

"You're not German, are you, Morley?" Murphy said. "I mean, it's funny an Irishman like yourself getting mixed up with this Kraut Guenther."

"Hans Guenther is an anti-communist," Paul said. "That's an idea you can get behind, no matter what country you came from."

"Do you support this man Hitler?" Latham said.

"I think he's got some good ideas," Paul said.

"Like invading Poland?" Murphy said. "You think that's a good idea?" He pointed to the headline on the newspaper in Latham's lap.

Paul shifted uncomfortably in his seat. "I don't know much about that. . . I just saw the headline this morning. . . I was going to call Hans and see what he could tell me."

Murphy snorted. "You'll have a hard time doing that, Morley. Your boy Hans Guenther has disappeared."

"What do you mean?"

"He's gone. We paid a visit to his apartment early this morning, and he was gone, vanished, he and the woman he lives with. The landlady couldn't tell us where he went. You wouldn't have another address for him, would you, Morley?"

Paul felt like he'd been hit with a sledgehammer. Hans gone? And Trudy was gone also. It couldn't be. It didn't make sense.

He tried to cover his disbelief with bravado. "Listen, I don't know a thing about that. Now, would you fellows please tell me what this is all about? It's not right to come in here and start firing questions at me without giving me an explanation."

"Sure, Morley, we'll tell you," Murphy said. "Hans Guenther is suspected of being an agent of the German government. He's a very clever fellow, though, and we haven't been able to pin anything on him as yet. But what we do know is that he's been embezzling funds from that German American Fraternal Society you're mixed up in, and he's been doing it for years. He's a thief and a swindler, and you're a damned fool for getting mixed up with him."

"What?" Paul said. "That's ridiculous. You'd better have some proof, Mr. Murphy. I trust Hans completely."
"Oh, we have proof," Murphy said. "We have lots of that. That's why we were after him this morning. We have enough proof to put him away for several years. And by the way, Morley, I wouldn't go anywhere, if I was you. We have auditors coming in here shortly to go over your books with a fine-toothed comb, and there could be lots of questions for you. Anyone who lets Hans Guenther handle their finances is in for a lot of suspicion. He's a master at embezzling funds."

"This is outrageous," Paul said, standing up. "And if you have nothing more than a bunch of accusations, I'll ask you to leave. I have a busy day ahead of me, and I don't have time for this."

"Sure," Murphy said. "We'll leave. But I'd watch yourself, fellow. With what Hitler just did, German American organizations like yours are going to come under a lot of scrutiny. You're in trouble, Mr. Morley, and you'd better watch yourself."

He stood up and turned on his heel, and Latham followed him out. Paul watched them go, and somehow he knew instinctively that what Murphy had said about Guenther was true. He looked out the window at his new building and realized that Duncan Paper Mill, the only place he'd ever worked, was headed for disaster.

CHAPTER ELEVEN

December 1943

"I never liked snow," Rose said. "To be sure, we never had much of it in the old country, but when it came something bad always happened. One time my mother wandered off in a snowstorm, bewitched by the quiet and stillness of the fairy dust, as she called it, and we found her the next day, shivering in a field a mile away. She nearly died that time, and she spent a week in bed, raving from her fevered visions, till it passed."

She was helping Martin with his coat and hat that morning, casting a worried eye at the gently falling snow outside the window. She had already told him that he was foolish to go to work on a day like this. "You're past 80 years old. Why can't you take a rest like other people? You're too old to be out and about in weather like this, Martin."

He had laughed like he always did when she scolded him, and said, "Too old? Why, Rose, I feel like a mere stripling, a boy of 18, especially when I look at those lively green eyes of yours. They give me the same feeling I had when I first met you, and I was just a boy then. Here, give me a kiss to warm me before I go out in the elements."

He leaned over and Rose kissed him, and he felt the same tingle, the same starburst of happiness, that he'd felt the first time she kissed him so many years ago in her rented room when he visited her after Peter had abandoned her.

"Saints preserve us, but you're full of blarney today," she said, pulling away after a moment. "Martin, I think you have Irish blood in you, the way you talk." She stared into his eyes. "I don't know what I'd do without you, you old coot, and that is why I worry when you don't listen to my advice."

"Don't worry, I won't be long," he said. "I just have a few clients to meet with, some documents to look at, and a hearing or two to get out of the way. And my clients don't call me 'old coot', by the way. They're very respectful to me, unlike you, my dear."

"Oh, tosh," she said, pulling his scarf tighter around his neck. "Be off with you, then. But don't stay long. If this snow keeps falling, the trolleys will stop running, and then you'll be stuck."

Martin went out with a spring in his step, the way he always did when Rose kissed him goodbye. He had never stopped feeling he was the luckiest man in the world – how wonderful it was that things worked out so he married the woman he fell in love with at 18.

Outside the sky was iron gray and heavy with snow, and there was already more than an inch of it on the sidewalk, although the street was clear. The snow felt like little icy kisses on his face as he walked to the trolley stop. When the trolley came he was grateful to get inside its warm cocoon, and he felt lucky to get a seat by a window, because the car was crowded due to gas rationing. People were taking more public transportation since the war started, because they could only get a limited amount of gasoline for their automobiles.

Martin settled into his seat and looked out at the city passing by. He had always enjoyed snowstorms, when the familiar cityscape changed into something strange and magical as the snow coated everything.

But that was not entirely a good thing, because familiarity was safety to him these days. His eyes were getting worse all the time, and his world was sharply marked by what he knew and didn't know. Anything new was a danger, and he stayed within the confines of the world he'd known for so many years. His memory had sharp pictures in it, even if his eyes could sometimes see only the blurry outlines of shapes.

It was getting harder to do his job, and nowadays he relied on help from various clerks to do his reading. He had not made much money in his legal career but he was respected around the courthouse, and there was no shortage of people willing to help him.

How long can I go on like this, though? he wondered. Rose hasn't had a real job in years; she's back to making her lace christening dresses just to earn a few dollars. I have almost nothing in the bank. If my health gets worse, we'll have nothing to live on.

He couldn't count on Paul to help them out, that was for sure. Paul was away in prison, thanks to his involvement with Hans Guenther and his German American Fraternal Society. It had been a disaster for Paul to get involved with that man on the eve of a world war, and it almost broke Rose's heart when her son was sentenced to prison.

Martin would not do anything unethical to help Paul, but he always suspected that someone behind the scenes had been looking out for him, because Paul was only charged with embezzlement, and got away with a relatively light five-year sentence for what he'd done.

He'd lost everything, though -- his company was bankrupt, his big house was gone, his wife and children were living in a tiny row house in the city now. Rose still visited him in prison regularly, but neither Lucy nor the children had been there, so far as Martin knew.

These were bad times. It sometimes seemed like the world had gone crazy, the whole world ablaze with war and destruction, and Martin couldn't understand how hatred had triumphed so completely. Why, it didn't make any sense how Paul, the child of an immigrant, could get mixed up with a philosophy that talked about the need for racial purity, and the hierarchy of the nations. He had shared the stage with a man who believed that some people were inferior to others, and that the world needed to be run by the superior races. It was madness, and Martin still thought that Paul didn't really believe it in his heart, that it was just blindness and vanity that made him do what he did.

The trolley screeched to a stop in front of the brick courthouse, and Martin got off. There was a hissing noise from the electric wires above the trolley, and a heavy electrical smell. Martin stepped right in a puddle and his shoes got soaked. Rubber was in short supply, and snow boots had just about vanished in the last few years, so Martin had nothing to protect his feet from the snow and slush that was pooling in the gutter. He winced as he pulled his feet from the puddle, and he shuffled across the street to the courthouse.

Inside, he went to his usual spot, which was nothing more than a coat hook on a wall, a plain wooden chair and a table in a corner where he could spread out his papers. There was a squat iron coal stove that kept the room pleasantly warm, and Martin was thankful for that.

He spent his day meeting with a column of raggedy clients, all of them facing petty charges, everything from public drunkenness to prostitution to check kiting. It had been years since he'd defended anything as serious as a person accused of murder, and he was thankful for it -- he did not think he had the energy anymore to take on a defense like that.

The people today all proclaimed their innocence, as usual, and he bantered with them the way he liked to do, telling them he'd gotten his legal degree from a drugstore around the corner, asking their opinion about how the baseball teams, the Phillies and Athletics, would do next season, and slipping them a few dollars to get a meal if they seemed underfed. The last one was a tall, cadaverous man named Billy Jenkins, who had come from a wealthy family like Martin and had been in the same social circles as a lad, although he'd left that world many years before when he developed too fond a taste for alcohol.

His path had crossed Martin's before, because his need for alcohol had driven him to try many illegal means of getting the money for a drink, including petty theft, posing as a door to door fundraiser for a charity, stealing cars, pimping, and passing himself off as an English nobleman so that he could prey on lonely old ladies and siphon off money from their bank accounts.

"Martin, you old rascal, how are you?" Billy said, sitting across from Martin, smiling raffishly despite his sunken cheeks and yellowish eyes and slovenly appearance.

"I'm fine," Martin said. "But how about you? You look like you slept in an alleyway, Billy."

"When the situation warrants it I've been known to take my rest out of doors," Billy said. "Nothing wrong with a little fresh air from time to time."

"That's not a healthy way to live," Martin said. "You know better than that. And we're not at an age where we should be doing such things."

Billy smiled, revealing gaps in his teeth. "Now, now, Martin, I appreciate your concern, but I'm not a man who is under the delusion that he will live forever. Have you ever heard of William Allingham, the Irish poet?"

"Can't say I have," Martin said.

"I'm a great lover of poetry, as you know, and he has a poem called, 'Twilight Voices' that expresses my sentiments very well." He leaned back in his chair. "Let's see, it goes like this:

Now, at the hour when ignorant mortals

Drowse in the shade of their whirling sphere,

Heaven and Hell from invisible portals

Breathing comfort and ghastly fear,

Voices I hear;

I hear strange voices, flitting, calling,

Wavering by on the dusky blast,--

'Come, let us go, for the night is falling;

Come, let us go, for the day is past!'"

Billy squinted in concentration. "Now how does it end? Oh yes. . .

See, I am ready, Twilight voices!

Child of the spirit-world am I;

How should I fear you? my soul rejoices,

O speak plainer! O draw nigh!

Fain would I fly!

Tell me your message, Ye who are calling

Out of the dimness vague and vast;

Lift me, take me,--the night is falling;

Quick, let us go,--the day is past.

"I love the spiritual aspect of Irish poetry, don't you?" Billy said. "It makes one feel better about the prospect of one's imminent demise, wouldn't you say?"

"Imminent demise?" Martin said, laughing. "Nonsense, Billy! I think you're indestructible. You'll be around for years."

"There comes a time for all of us," Billy said, wagging his finger, "when we cast off our mortal coils, as it were. We've had a good run, Martin. And, if you don't mind my saying, you're looking a bit gray in the cheek. I have a good reason for appearing this way, you know. You, however, are a respectable citizen with a wife who takes care of you. You don't have an excuse."

"It's just my age," Martin said. "It's natural for us, Billy. We're both over 80, and we're supposed to look this way."

"Well, I've looked this way since I was 25," Billy said. "It's not age, it's the effects of bad living. I repeat that you don't have that excuse, old man. You're not supposed to look like me."

"Do you need a place to stay?" Martin said. "Or a good meal? Rose makes a very good meat loaf dinner, as you know."

"Thank you, but no," Billy said. "Most nights, I've got a bed in the St. Agnes Mission on Fitzwater Street. They feed me pretty well, and I only have to listen to a Bible verse or two as payment for my lodging. I highly recommend it."

"Suit yourself," Martin said.

Billy pointed to the window and said, "By the way, old man, you may want to get home before that storm gets any worse. It's coming down in sheets now and I doubt the public transport will be running much longer." He stood up. "We're finished here, aren't we? If you don't mind, I'd like to set sail for Fitzwater Street. Don't want to keep the good sisters waiting."

He shuffled off in his loose-limbed gait, and Martin turned to the window, where he could see the snow coming down much harder.

He gathered his papers together and put them in his briefcase, then put on his overcoat and scarf and headed downstairs. He was having difficulty walking today, his legs feeling like they were made of cement, and he was breathing hard with every step. I must get in to see my doctor soon, he thought again. Probably nothing serious, but I'd better check just in case.

Outside, the snow was coming down furiously, and it had turned from sleet to hard little pellets of ice that stung when they hit you. Martin had to squint into the wind to see where he was going, and it was only from memory that he found his way to the trolley stop, where a small knot of people stood, shivering as they waited.

It was dead calm. There were no cars on the street, and the sky was a pearl gray color, reflecting the lights from the nearby buildings and giving everything an eerie glow. The voices in the small group waiting at the trolley stop seemed to die out as soon as they spoke, muffled by the blanket of snow. There was at least seven inches of snow on the ground now, and it seemed to be falling faster.

Martin smelled the trolley before he saw it, the electric smell acrid in his nostrils. It screeched to a stop and he got on, grateful to be able to sit and catch his breath. He listened to the snow beating against the window, and he got suddenly scared, as if he was unmoored for a moment. What if the trolley breaks down and I'm trapped? I can't see well in this storm, and I won't know where I am. Rose will worry about me.

Rose. Her face swam into his vision as the trolley lurched along its way. He could not believe his luck that he'd found her. What if she'd stayed married to that Peter Morley, or what if she'd moved back to Ireland? I would have never seen her again, never had the chance to love her the way I've done for all these years. I'd have stayed at my father's law firm and had a boring, miserable life, never known that there was a part of my heart waiting to open like a flower. The girl I'd fallen in love with at 18 would have walked out of my life, and I would have lived out my days with an impoverished heart.

It had been worth it, every minute of it. He knew that old friends looked at him with pity, and he could sometimes hear the murmuring behind his back when he passed them in the courtroom corridors. "I went to school with him," they'd say. "Now look at him, the poor fellow. Wears shoes with holes in them and has patches on his elbows." He knew they thought he was crazy for giving up the patrimony that was his, the Lancaster wealth and family name, the respectability, the power. He was a lesson to them, an object lesson in what could happen if you let love rule you, instead of good sense.

He smiled to himself when he heard their comments. I'm the lucky one, he thought. I made it out of that stifling, choking life, that life of artificiality, of shallow chumminess and club ties and summers in Maine and love affairs to cover up the loneliness. I found a real, deep love, one that has brightened every day of my life.

I must tell Rose how much she means to me, he thought. He was not a demonstrative person; it was a trait of his class not to show emotion. He wished he could write poetry, something beautiful to give her. She had been such a blessing, such a gift. He decided he'd tell her that; it had been too long since he'd told her the depth of his feelings.

The trolley was almost empty now; people had been getting off at stops along the way, but nobody had gotten on. It was five o'clock and businesses were already closed; people were staying home in their warm houses, rather than going out. There were a few lone cars on the street, but mostly it was empty.

He was troubled by the fact that his breathing had not gotten better even though he was sitting. Usually when he had these spells it was because he had walked up a flight of steps, or moved in too much of a hurry. It was puzzling that he was seated and yet his breath was still labored.

Next week, I'll call Doc Fisher. He'll fix me up in no time.

Martin knew the trolley was coming up to his stop, and he thought happily that Rose would meet him at the door and help him get his coat off, then make him sit down in front of the fireplace and drink a steaming mug of tea. It was a thought that brought a smile to his face.

When the trolley lurched to a stop, Martin got out of his seat and shuffled down the steps and out the door. The snow was still coming down hard, and the temperature had dropped sharply, so that Martin gasped from the sudden cold. The trolley doors closed and it groaned and moved forward, and Martin looked around to get his bearings.

Everything was gray, with the light coming from everywhere and nowhere. There were streetlights above, but they were shrouded in the gray mist and the thick snowfall. When the trolley left there was a sudden, all-encompassing silence, no sound at all. Martin stepped off the curb, but he could not see to the other side of the street, and he was not really sure what direction he was going in.

Then he heard Rose's voice. "Martin, are you over there? I came out to meet you."

"I'm here my darling," he called. "But how did you know I was coming now?"

"I had a feeling," she said. "Something told me to come out. Don't ask questions, now, Martin. It's cold and I want you to come inside."

"I'll be right across," he called. "Thank you for coming." He was grateful for the sound of her voice, and he started across the street in the direction that he had heard the voice coming from.

He was halfway there, and he could just see the outline of Rose through the mist, clad in her maroon raincoat and holding a black umbrella, when he heard a car coming. It was coming fast, from the sound of it, and the engine roared against the backdrop of silence all around. He could not see it, and he did not know even what direction it was coming from.

"Hurry, Martin," Rose called. "I hear a car coming." Her arm was stretched out to him, and he wanted nothing more than to get to it, but his body felt so heavy and sluggish, and it was hard to get his breath. He tried to get his legs to move, but it was like he was walking in wet cement. He was afraid of falling, too, so he dare not move too fast.

The car was closer now, and the roar of the engine was deafening. Martin figured the driver would see him soon, and put on the brakes. He won't hit me, Martin thought. I can be sure of that.

The headlights had already appeared, and Martin was blinded by their ferocious brightness. He felt as if he were surrounded by light, lost in a bubble of blinding luminescence.

"Martin!" Rose said. "You're going the wrong way. Turn toward me."

He realized he had turned around and was heading straight toward the headlights. He turned toward Rose's voice and took a step, but now the car appeared. He saw it as a dark shape at the edge of his vision, with headlights like the eyes of some great beast, coming fast.

Everything seemed to move in slow motion then. He heard the driver slam on the car's brakes, and the squealing sound as they tried to stop the car. There was a swishing sound of tires sliding on the snow, a voice cursing at him, and the last thing, the very last thing was the sound of Rose's scream, her wailing, lost, bereft scream that pierced his being just before the front of the car hit him and he went flying through the air.

And there was nothing more.

CHAPTER TWELVE

January 6, 1944

To Paul Morley

Leavenworth Prison

Paul:

It agonizes me to write these words, but I must tell you that my dear Martin has died. He is gone, Paul, the man who loved me since I was barely 20 years old. I do not know how I will bear this loss.

He died last week, and is already buried. He was crossing the street in the middle of a snowstorm, right in front of me, and he was hit by a car. His eyes were bad, as you know, getting worse all the time, and he did not see the car until it was too late. The driver drove off into the night without stopping.

It is like a gentle light has gone out of the world, and I am plunged into darkness. Martin was a rock for me to hold onto in the most perilous times, and I would not have survived this long without him.

I have never known a kinder man than Martin Lancaster. He never thought of himself, only others. He never insisted on any special treatment, although he was born into a world that demanded it for people of his class. He could have married one of the debutantes he went to school with and worked his whole life in one of the old-line Philadelphia law firms, belonging to all the best clubs and living in a house on the Main Line. That was the path that was expected of him, but instead he spent his life working for people who had nothing, defending the outcasts of society, who had no one to stand up for them.

Money and class meant nothing to him. He gave all of that up when he married me. His parents disowned him and yet he never regretted it. There are times when I wake up in the middle of the night and wonder how I ever deserved him.

Martin taught me that that all people have dignity, Paul. He saw the good in everyone, even the prostitutes and con artists and swindlers he defended. He didn't think anyone was above anyone else. He taught me more about love than any priest or preacher I've ever met.

I do not know how I will survive, but I know that somehow I will. The human soul is stronger than we think.

I hope you understand that, and that your present predicament does not make you lose heart.

You seemed sad the last time I visited you, and I hope things are better now. You must try to keep your spirits up. It is the best way to get through a bad situation.

I know it is not easy being in prison, but you must think of the bright side. The lawyers say that you were in serious danger of being deported for treasonous activity, because of your involvement with Hans Guenther and that organization he got you mixed up in. This is wartime, and because Guenther and his people were telling young men not to register for the draft, you were a party to treasonous acts. If not for dear Martin, whose friends in the justice system respected him and looked out for you, you would have been charged with much worse crimes than embezzlement.

I know it seems unjust that you were even charged with that, and you have proclaimed your innocence many times, saying that you never took any money from the company, and that Guenther was lying when he said you were involved. Maybe that is true, but five years in prison for the crime of embezzlement is much better than being deported for treason, to my way of thinking.

Yes, the paper company that you spent so many years with is now bankrupt, and I am sure that is a bitter pill. You will have to find other work when you are released from prison, and try to rebuild your life.

I know that Lucy does not visit you, so you have no news about how your family is doing. She had to sell the big house in Cheltenham, and she and the children moved to a modest twin house in West Philadelphia, near where we used to live when you were a boy. She has found a job as a secretary with a firm in the city, and that helps to put food on the table for them.

I hope and pray that you will be able to mend the problems you have caused for her and the children. Their hearts are broken, and you will have to fix that.

For of all the things you did, Paul, all the mistakes you made, perhaps the biggest is that you shattered your family. I do not understand what you were looking for with that other woman, but whatever she gave you could not have been enough to break up your home.

What was going through your mind? Family is the most precious thing we have, it is the root of our existence. We must preserve it at all costs. I wanted to keep my family back in Ireland together, but I lost them all. The family I started here has had its hardships, and sometimes seems ready to fade out like a sputtering candle.

    You and Lucy and the children are all I have left, Paul, and I want you to stay together. It is a precious thing, your family, and I do not want to see you lose it.

    That's what puzzles me about what happened to you. I don't understand how you could get mixed up with someone like Hans Guenther in the first place. All that nonsense about some races being better than others; how could you ever be a party to that, Paul? Did I not tell you over and over about all the misery caused by that attitude back in the old country? The English acted like we were an inferior race, and even when we tried to come here and start a new life, those attitudes followed us here. When I first came here there were places that would not hire Irish people. They made fun of us on the stage, as if we were a lower form of life.

    I wanted something better for my family, and that is why I came here. And I met many other people who came here for the same reason. This country was built by people looking to get away from those old attitudes in the countries they came from. People like Hans Guenther are just trying to bring the Old World's problems over here.

    Paul, I expected better from you. You are the child of an immigrant. I know you felt like an outsider in your life. We were shunned by the other Irish who lived around us, because of the unfortunate circumstances of Tim's birth. When your father left us, things turned even worse. We had no money, and it was a hard life. I know you felt like an outcast yourself, a boy without a father, and maybe that is what spurred you to make something of yourself.

I suppose you felt like you had finally been admitted to the club when you raised yourself up to a position of prominence. You had a grand big house, a fancy car, and you knew rich and powerful people.

But that is not what matters in this life. How many of those people came to your defense when you were in trouble? How many have visited you in prison? Not many, I am sure. The world you belonged to was a false and shallow one, Paul, and those people cared no more for you than they did for a gardener or a chauffeur in their employ.

These are desperate times, my son. The war has made us all realize how fragile our lives are. Everyone is feeling like the ground under their very feet is ready to give way. The news from Europe gets worse every day, and we wonder what will come of all this fighting. The only solace is to have faith that love will win out in the end. Love is what truly matters in life, Paul. Cling to that.

You have a job to do when you get out of prison, and that is to go back and mend things with your family. They need you desperately, even if they do not realize it now. Rosie especially seems to need a father in her life. It is hard for Lucy to control her, and she spends her time running around with musicians and sneaking in to nightclubs. She needs your guidance, Paul. So does Billy, who is 12 now, and needs a man to show him how to live the right way.

I know you probably think you have ruined your life, that you have trampled on your family and all is lost. It would be easy to feel despair now, but do not.

I have been through many low points in my life, and despair has been a companion of mine many times. When I was a child my mother was touched in the head. She would speak to us of fairies and witches and the Good People, and although I loved her very much I could not understand her, and she scared me very much. She would disappear for days on end, and when she came back she would be talking about the magical places she'd been to, and the strange creatures she'd seen. It was not a proper childhood for me, with a proper mother. She wormed her way into my dreams, into the lonely places inside my soul, and I have never really recovered from knowing her. She lived through the Great Famine, and she was never right afterward. My father told me she had seen her own mother die of hunger, and it broke her mind like a porcelain bowl that's been shattered into a thousand shards.

Added to that, I grew up in a land that was racked with anguish, a land where people could not own the land they had lived on for generations. We were desperately poor, barefoot, and hungry most of the time. We dressed in rags and barely had any schooling; we were like wild animals when I think of it now. There were times even as a child when I was denied the happiness that should be a child's portion, when I lay awake at night and wondered if sadness was all there was in life, sadness and desperation and screaming agony sometimes.

Even with all the sadness it was brutally hard to tear myself away when I was 18 and come to America. I left behind my family, and everything I had ever known, to come to this strange, big, bustling country. I saw things that I could hardly believe, and there was much to wonder at, but I was also lonely and homesick and cried myself to sleep some nights. Still, I got through it, and I had a measure of happiness, especially in the beginning with your father.

Ah, your father. There was no man who could light up a room like that one. He had a smile like sunshine, a body like a lumberjack, and a voice like a trumpet pealing out the sounds of God's coming. He was like fireworks every day for me.

He could not stay still, though, and he could not stay true. He could not tell the truth to save his life, and so he was not a man to spend your life with. It crushed me and almost killed me when he left, but in the years since I have realized that it was for the best. It would have killed me if he'd stayed around, and it would have poisoned your life. He was not made to be a husband or father, of that I am sure.

So, I trudged on, putting one foot in front of the other, and I just kept going. I could not let the sadness pull me down. I thought if I kept going I would somehow get to the end, find some measure of happiness at the end of the journey. When your brothers died, however, I almost gave up. I could see Tim's death coming, sad as it was, but poor Willy's passing was so sudden it almost did me in. If it weren't for Martin's strong arms holding me up I would have surely fallen down in my tracks.

So, I have survived all these hardships in my 80 years, but now Martin is gone. At times in the last week I have found myself wondering if I will be joining him soon. I do not know how I can go on without him in my life. Somehow, though, I know I must. That is the point, Paul -- we must keep going, no matter what. God has a plan for us, I am convinced of that, even though we don't see it in our blindness.

You must go on. You must find a way to win Lucy and your family back, and be the husband and father you were meant to be. You will find a way, I am sure. Think about it now, while you are alone. Pray about it. Make a plan. You must and will make up for your mistakes, Paul. They will not bring you down.

Keep going.

Love,

Your mother Rose

CHAPTER THIRTEEN

December 21, 1944

"I have another big test in History, Mom," Rosie said, stuffing her schoolbooks into her bag as she hurried to get out the front door. "I'm going to Jane Wilson's house again to study. I won't be back till late."

"Again?" her mother said from upstairs. "I thought you just had a test last week. How many tests does this teacher give?"

"I told you before, he believes in giving a lot of tests. I have to do well in this class. You don't want me to flunk, do you?"

"Why can't your friend Jane ever come here?" her mother said. "You're always going over to her house."

"Mom, it's just easier this way. She has a sick mother who gets worried if she's out too late."

"Well, I'm not sick, but I worry about you being out too late also."

"Mom! I'll take the bus home, like always. You know it's safe. I have to go. Bye!"

Rosie ran out the door and down the steps, then raced down the driveway toward the bus stop a block away. The bus came in five minutes, and she got on and sat in the back, like always. Two stops later Jane got on.

"Are you ready?" Jane said, sitting next to her. "I heard there's a big destroyer in at the Navy base, and there will be a lot of sailors at the USO tonight."

"The more the better," Rosie said. "I can't wait to try out that 'Rum And Coca Cola' number. I've been practicing it all week."

"You're so bad," Jane said. "The words to that are risque, aren't they?"

"Oh, that just means people will pay extra close attention to my singing," Rosie said, laughing.

"You never have any problem with that," Jane said. "I see the way the boys look at you. They can't take their eyes off you. You look great on stage, and you sing like an angel. After the war, you should go into show business."

"Oh, I'm sure my mother would love that," Rosie said, rolling her eyes. "She'd have a stroke if she knew I was singing at the USO. Look at how I have to run around and hide all this from her. If she ever found out what I was doing she'd disown me."

Things weren't going well with her mother, but Rosie just couldn't be the girl she wanted her to be. She was too mad to be alive, too in love with the crazy energy all around her, to be the straitlaced, proper girl her mother wanted. She felt bad about that, because she knew how hard the last few years had been, and how devastated her mom had been after all that happened with her father. It just wasn't fair, though: she couldn't fit the mold her mother wanted her to fit, and no amount of sadness would change that.

They rode the bus all the way to the terminal at the bus station in the city, where they took their school bags and went straight to the Women's Room. They went in adjoining stalls and did a quick change from their Catholic school uniforms into the dresses they'd brought in their bags -- a green and white flowered dress for Jane, and a black cocktail dress with a sprinkling of sequins across the bodice for Rosie. She had made it herself in secret on her mother's sewing machine, and she set it off with a red rose in her ear and bright red lipstick, brushing her black hair across one eye like her favorite movie star, Veronica Lake.

When they were ready they walked to the USO club, which was on Sansom street in the city, in the middle of a rather seedy block of bars, barbershops and dry cleaners. The place was packed with servicemen, mostly sailors from the ship that had docked the day before. Rosie breezed over to the stage area at the back, went over her numbers with the musicians for a few minutes, then turned and waited for the MC, a staccato-talking Jimmy Cagney lookalike, to introduce her.

She closed her eyes and launched into "Stardust", letting the music overwhelm her the way it always did. It had a power, this music, to sweep everything along with it on a current of love. The world was a better place when she was singing. It was amazing, because she had only discovered this voice a few years ago. She had always loved to sing, but after she had a bout with rheumatic fever at the age of 13 something changed. She suddenly had a woman's voice, a big throaty voice that had power and vulnerability in it all at once.

It was a voice that compelled her to sing, and she sang whenever she had the chance -- in church, at amateur contests, and when she discovered that the USO was looking for singers for its servicemen's club, she found her way to them and lied about her age so they would hire her to sing once a week, as she had been doing for the last year. The manager of the club looked astounded when he asked her to audition and she crooned "A String Of Pearls", and even the jaded members of the band applauded when she sang the last note.

Now, when she was finished the servicemen clapped, some of them looking moved by her voice. She put all her emotion into her singing, all her longing and pain and loneliness, but also her love of life, and she could see in people's eyes that it affected them.

There was an officer sitting right in the front row who caught her eye, and her next number, "Begin the Beguine" she sang directly to him. He was a lean, rangy man in his late twenties, and he had deep brown eyes with hurt in them, and also pain. He was wearing a British officer's uniform, with a row of ribbons on his chest. He looked straight at her the whole time.

When they begin

the beguine

it brings back the sound

of music so tender

it brings back a night

of tropical splendor

it brings back a memory of green. . .

When she finished he smiled at her, and then he kept that smile on his face for the rest of the songs in her set. She stared straight back at him and sang her heart out again and again, and she knew when she finished her set he'd want to talk to her. When she finished she didn't even wait to hear all the applause -- she stepped down off the stage and went straight over to him.

He stood up like a gentleman, and she wondered what a British serviceman was doing here in Philadelphia. She guessed he had some connection to the Navy Yard nearby. She had heard that some British ships were brought in for repairs, and maybe he was with one of them.

"Your voice is smashing," he said, pulling out a chair for her.

"Thank you," she said, sitting down. "Do you have a cigarette?"

"Certainly." He pulled out a gold case, opened it, and selected two cigarettes. He lit one with an engraved gold lighter, then gave it to her. He put the second cigarette in his mouth and lit that one, exhaling a long stream of smoke.

"How did you learn to sing like that, if I may ask?" he said.

"I never took lessons," she said. "I just always loved to sing. It comes naturally, I guess."

"You're a bit young to be on stage, aren't you?" he smiled, and it was a crooked, boyish smile that contrasted with the crinkled lines around the edges of his eyes.

"How young do you think I am?" she said, exhaling smoke.

"Young enough that you're trying to impress me with your sophistication with that cigarette, but you've obviously never smoked before."

"What do you mean?" she said. "I smoke all the time."

"I see, that explains the very sophisticated way you're dropping ashes in my drink," he said.

"Oh, I'm sorry," she said, blushing deeply. "I didn't realize. . ." she was so flustered she took an extra big drag of her cigarette, and then she got a coughing fit, which lasted a full minute.

The man grabbed a glass of water from a nearby table and made her drink it. When she finally got herself under control, she said, "Thank you." She stubbed the cigarette out in an ashtray. "I shouldn't be smoking these anyway. Bad for my voice."

"So, do you want to be a professional singer?" he said.

"I would love that," she said. "I know all the popular songs, and people tell me I sing like Peggy Lee. When the war is over I'm going to go up to New York and get an agent, find a band to sing with. I'll be famous, just like Frankie Sinatra. You'll see."

"You have it all planned out, eh? Well, that's tiptop. Nothing like a bit of hope for the future."

"Don't you have hope?" she said. "After all, it looks like the war will be over sometime soon. We're licking the Germans and the Japanese. We'll have this thing all cleaned up in no time."

He smiled. "I admire your enthusiasm; I'm not so sure I share it, though. The world is an evil place. Just because the Allies win the war doesn't mean things will suddenly turn all sunny and bright."

"Oh, don't be such a stick in the mud. There's no reason to take such a dim view of things. Why, it's a time to be happy, don't you think?"

"I wish I could be happy," he said, taking a drag of his cigarette. "I've seen a bit too much to be happy. Too many friends lost, too many bad scenes I've witnessed up close."

"You sound English. What are you doing in Philadelphia?"

"I'm here with a ship. I'm overseeing the repairs to HMS Reliant, a destroyer. I've never been to Philadelphia before. Seems like a nice place."

"You're new in town?" Rosie said. "Then I need to show you around. I have to go back and do two more sets, but when I'm done let's go outside and see the Christmas lights on City Hall."

"Sounds lovely."

She sang the next two sets as if she had an audience of one -- him. She let the music take her, the emotions playing out on her face, using every color in her vocal palette to paint a picture of lushness, romance, high spirits.

When she finished the last song the crowd applauded enthusiastically, and she acknowledged them, but she had one goal in mind. She went over to him and took his hand, and he helped her with her coat and then they went outside to the clear, cold night and walked toward the City Hall building, glowing in the night like a big wedding cake decorated with multi-colored candles.

She felt so alive, so excited she did not think she could ever sleep again. There was something magical in the air, and she talked nonstop, telling him everything about her life, her hopes, her dreams. She wanted to talk forever, to stay up all night, to sing, to laugh, to run and jump and dance.

Somehow they ended up in an alleyway across from City Hall, and as carolers sang "Joy To The World" she pressed against him and lost herself in a deep and melting kiss. His lips were the sweetest she had ever tasted, and her heart raced as his gentle fingers ran through her hair, brushing against her cheek, stopping to caress her breast through the buttons of her coat, and making her breath go shallow and ragged. She felt snowflakes falling on her neck but they melted instantly as her skin heated up. They kissed for what seemed like hours, and when they finally broke apart, she heard herself say, in a ragged voice, "Do that again."

And he did. This time he took her in his arms more boldly, pressing her against the wall, and his mouth went to hers with an insistent pulsing heat. He had one hand around her waist and the other at her shoulder blades, and he pulled her to him with almost a desperate intensity. He was desperate, it was true, like a hungry man is desperate for a meal, but he was also supremely sure of himself, a man who had seen and done a lot in his short lifetime. He kissed her eyelids, her cheek, her neck, behind her ear, each time sending her into greater and greater ecstasies.

It was like a fevered dream, a reverie or a meditation. She was in another world, a world of grace and light and energy that radiated from him, from her, from everywhere. He was murmuring things in her ear, syllables half heard and she replied in her own strange language that he somehow understood. It was a communion of bodies and spirits on the streets of the city, with snow falling like silent caresses and Christmas carolers filling the spaces between the snowflakes. Time stopped, or rather it became utterly meaningless, an absurd little exercise in counting that had no connection to what was happening between them. She felt on the verge of a swoon, on the edge of a sheer drop into the unknown, the void yawning below. She was standing at the rim of a volcano, peering into the trackless darkness below, feeling the hot breeze on her face and wondering "Should I?"

He ran his hand up under her dress and she trembled with wanting, felt her nerves vibrate like the strings of a cello, felt her breath stop and her heart jump in her chest. She had been with other boys, lots of them, because she had always been curious and had an explorer's heart. They were like treasures in an old trunk you'd find in an attic, pretty shiny things that you held up to the light for a moment and then discarded, in search of something newer.

This one, though, was different. He had eyes that held you steady, a smile that knew your secrets, lips that worked magic and hands that were like a sculptor's. There was no getting around it: he was someone you'd stop your life for.

It occurred to her that she didn't know his name. That had not always been important before, but suddenly it was now.

"What is your name?" she whispered. "Mine's Rosie."

"My name?" he said. "It's Charlesworth. James Charlesworth."

CHAPTER FOURTEEN

July 4, 1945.

"The Charlesworth men have been in the English military for generations," James said, looking out at the Schuykill River meandering by, the sun glinting off it like shards of bright glass. "That's why it was such a shock to my father when I wanted to join the Navy. I always loved the water, though."

He was holding Rosie's hand as they sat on the bank of the river, eating a picnic lunch that Rosie had packed, while the soft July breeze cooled their faces. There were scattered oarsmen plying their sport here and there, and there were flocks of pigeons and seagulls squawking over food morsels left by picnickers earlier in the day.

Rosie was happier than she'd ever been. He was so handsome in his officer's uniform, and she felt lucky to have met him. So this was love, she felt. This was the feeling that would lead people to do crazy things. Perhaps this was what her father was feeling when he kissed that German woman in the grape arbor so long ago. It was dangerous and thrilling and disturbing all at once.

"Just look at that water," James was saying. "Isn't it amazing, Rosie? It's so calming, yet it never stops moving. Do you see? It keeps flowing along on its way. We try to dam it, divert it, control it, but we can never really stop it, can we? It's like the flow of Time, I suppose. It simply goes on, and we are carried along by it. The trick is to enjoy the ride, isn't it?"

"Yes," Rosie said. "And I've been enjoying every minute of it. This war has taught me the value of living for the moment."

It was true. Sometimes it seemed as though a whole lifetime had been compressed into these last few years. She had started the war as a girl of 13, but now she was a woman of 18. She had experienced love, deep, sensual love at the hands of this dashing British officer, and she felt forever changed.

"I am fortunate that the stream of my life has brought me here," James said. "To meet you. Just think, if not for the war, I'd have never come to Philadelphia. It was just a happenstance that I was in a position to be asked to come here and oversee the repairs to one of our ships in your Navy Yard. I could have ended up in a hundred other places. I could be stuck on an aircraft carrier in the Sea of Japan right now, dodging kamikaze planes as they fly into the ship."

He opened a sandwich from the picnic basket and bit into it. It was sardines on white bread with some olives she had found in her mother's icebox, all that was available with food rationing, but he acted as if it were caviar. He picked up another sandwich and held it out to her, but she felt a wave of nausea, and shook her head no.

"Not hungry?" he said.

"Maybe later," she replied. "My stomach is a little queasy."

"What a perfect day," he said. "I can't think of anything that would make it better."

She decided the moment was right. She reached out and took his hand. "There is something that I think will make it even better," she said. "The cherry on top of the cake, James."

"What's that, darling?"

"I'm pregnant. We're going to have a baby."

His face changed. It was like a cloud passed over it. "What did you say?"

She squeezed his hand. "A baby. We're going to have a baby!"

"How do you know?"

"I've just been to the doctor yesterday. They say I'm two months pregnant. Isn't that great? It's probably from that night we were celebrating the end of the war in Europe. Remember, in May how everyone in your hotel was banging pots and pans and celebrating? That was quite a night. It was like Fourth of July and New Year's Eve and Christmas all rolled into one. Isn't this marvelous news?"

He looked at her dumbly, not seeming to understand.

"What's the matter?" she said. "Is something wrong?"

There was a long pause, during which she heard a mother calling to her child somewhere across the river.

"Rosie, I have to go back to England," he stammered. "The Pacific War will be over in a matter of weeks, um, a few months at the most. Then will come the task of rebuilding. England is my home, and I need to go back."

"Oh, I've already thought of that," Rosie said. "I can pack up and leave in no time. I don't have much to pack, really. I think it will be an adventure, you know. And I can't wait to meet your folks. You've told me so much about them, I feel like I already know

them. It will be great, won't it?"
He pulled his hand away from her.

"Rosie, that's not going to work."

"What do you mean?"

"Well, ah. . . I suppose I should have told you this before, but, well. . . I'm married."

She felt like she had fallen from a great height and had jarred herself, hitting her head on the ground. Her mind was suddenly working very slowly. "Wh, what did you say?"

His eyes looked pained. "I am, ah, married. Yes, married. I have a wife. A child too, actually. A boy named Jonathan. He'll be five years old in a few days."

"But that's ridiculous. You can't love her. You love me."

He took her hand, suddenly more assured. "Rosie, I am sorry about this, really I am. I meant to tell you. It's just, well, war is such a crazy thing. It turns everything upside down. I worried about my family constantly, worried about being killed or taken prisoner when I was on ship, worried after I got here about being so far from home, in such a strange place. I guess I buckled under pressure, you know. I didn't mean to do it, but I was feeling so lonely, so scared. You must understand, my darling. It was a wonderful affair while it lasted, but, well, it wasn't meant to go on forever. I have a family at home, and I miss them very much. You do understand, don't you?"

Rosie was numb, mute, stunned. She could not even shake her head yes or no. She simply sat there, with all her joy turned to ashes, wondering what she was going to do now.

"You must try to understand," he said. "I'll do the right thing, of course. We'll find you a doctor who can, ah, take care of that issue. We'll fix it all up, don't you worry. You're a young girl, Rosie, and you have your whole life ahead of you. This is just a momentary heartache, but you'll forget it in no time."

She could not think. He was talking to her, but it was gibberish, nonsense, like the Edward Lear nonsense poetry her mother read to her as a child. She felt like she was going to throw up, and she struggled to her feet to get away, because she did not want to do that in front of him. He reached for her arm but she recoiled from his touch.

"Don't," she said. "Don't touch me."

She stumbled off as he called after her, a pleading note in his voice. Suddenly she could not stand the sound of his voice, and she wanted to get as far away from him as possible.

She walked up the bank and onto the path, and kept walking, wanting to find some tree she could hide behind and vomit her guts out. He was calling still, a note of alarm in his voice, but she did not answer him, did not ever want to answer him again.

This could not be happening. She had thought they were in love, deeply in love. It was her first experience of love, of intimacy with a man, and she thought it was for the ages. The feeling of joy explained everything to her, the mysteries of adulthood were finally revealed to her. This was why people did crazy, stupid things and risked everything. Suddenly it all made sense. This was the most powerful force on Earth and now she had felt it and knew its power. She was ready to spend her life with him, to follow him to England or wherever his career took him. She would give up her dream of being a singer; that went without saying. It had been her only dream, the one thing she had always wanted, but she was ready to give it up without a thought.

Except he did not feel the same way.

He did not feel the same way.

This love she felt had not been earth shattering for him, not been the reason and ground of his existence, not explained the universe to him.

It had simply been a way for him to deal with his homesickness, nothing more. It was a drug, an anodyne to the heartsickness he felt at missing his family.

His family. He had other people he loved, a place in his heart that was barred to her, forever closed. She was a flirtation, a romp, a trifle, nothing more.

And she understood something else about adulthood, that the bitterness and anger and malice that so many of them had was due to this -- to having your heart cast aside like it was a toy in the hand of a child who was finished with it. Now she understood why so many people walked around with shriveled up faces and thin lips and narrow, sad eyes. Their hearts had been stung, had flowered once and then been shocked with a sudden frost and they were forever stunted; grotesque parodies of what a human heart should look like.

She lurched toward a willow tree on the riverbank, and grabbing one of its low-hanging branches she bent over and spewed out the contents of her stomach, retching till it felt like her very insides were coming out. The world spun around and around, and she felt as if she had to hold on or she'd go tumbling down the bank and into the river. Her eyes were tearing and her nose was running, and she could see gobs of the banana and cereal she'd had for breakfast on her skirt. This was about as horrible as it could get, she thought, but then there was a hand on her shoulder, and a whispery Irish voice: "Cha d'dhùin doras nach d'fhosgail doras. . . no door closed without another opening."

She turned and looked, but there was no one there, just a wind rustling through the trees.

That voice was one she'd heard before though. At night sometimes, on the edge of dreams, she had heard it -- an old, thin, whispery voice that beckoned. It was a voice that disturbed her, and she had often told it to go away as a child.

She shook her head to clear it, then straightened up and made her way along the riverbank to the Girard Avenue bridge, a sturdy edifice of gray stone and cast iron, with tall street lights lining it like black sentinels.

There were no cars on the bridge when she got there, and she went over to the iron railing and looked down at the river. It was wide at this point, like a brown highway to the tower of William Penn at City Hall in the distance. There were some rowers in the distance, lone figures on the scalloped surface of the water, and there was an explosion of noise as a flock of birds flew by overhead, on their way home before night came. She heard the clop clop of horses' hooves across the river, and saw two riders making their way along a path near the water's edge.

She had clarity about what she was doing to do. There was no other option now. It would be quick and painless, but necessary. There was no way she could go on now.

She checked to make sure no cars were coming, then hoisted herself up on the wrought iron railing, balancing precariously a hundred feet above the river. It would be a few seconds of being airborne, feeling the wonder of falling through space, and then oblivion in the brown water below.

"Bedad, now what have we here?" came a booming voice behind her.

She felt a viselike grip on her ankle, and looked around to see a big Irish policeman smiling up at her.

"Thinking of doing a bit of flying, are we?" he said. He had a bulbous nose with pockmarked skin, and his weathered face was split in a grin.

"Let me go," she said. "Go away. I want to do this."

"Do ye now?" he said. "I've often wondered meself what it would feel like to jump off this bridge, but I don't recommend it, actually. It tends to create quite a mess at the bottom. I've fished a few bodies out of this pond, young lady, and I have no desire to do it again. For one thing, I don't like getting me feet wet."

"Just leave, will you?" she said. "I made up my mind. I have no reason to live."

"Oh, that's what they all say," the policeman said. "But there's always a reason to live. If not for yourself, why, then for the other people in your life. We all have people who'd miss us if we left too early."

She wanted to just jump and be done with him, but his grip was like iron and she knew he'd pull her back up the minute she tried to go over the railing.

"I just want to die," she said, through her tears. "I've made a big mistake. I can't go on like this."

He chuckled, and his face broke into a new set of wrinkles. "Oh, we all make mistakes, Miss, that's something you need to learn. Why, the world runs on mistakes the way a car runs on gasoline. Take out the mistakes and you'd have a world that didn't go anywhere. Mistakes are what gives us hope."

"What are you talking about?" she said. "That doesn't make any sense at all."

"It's simple. None of us is perfect. We all make lots of mistakes. The way to look at it is we're all trying to get better, and the mistakes just show us that we still have a long way to go. Without mistakes, we'd have no vision of being better.

"And listen to me, young lady," he continued. "There's no man on earth worth jumping off this bridge for. Carrying some fellow's child are ye? Well, I hope ye'll think more about that life inside ye than the palooka who jilted ye. That baby's the important thing. Why, think how happy ye'll make your family when they see that little bundle of joy."

"Happy?" Rosie said. "They won't be happy at all. They'll be ashamed of me."

"Nonsense," he said. "Oh, they might feel that way for a moment, but I guarantee you they'll open their arms to a new babe. There's not a man nor woman on the planet who can resist the charms of one of them gifts from God. Why, it's an occasion for hope and joy. Don't you see that?"

"I can't tell them," Rosie said, weeping. "They'll be humiliated. They'll cut me out of their lives."

"Tosh," he said. "It's not as bad as all that. There's always someone you can tell. Come on now, girl, you must have someone. If not yer Ma, then yer Pa. Am I right? I'm sure the old man will be just tickled with this news."

"You are the craziest policeman I've ever met," Rosie shouted. "Don't you understand what I'm saying? I'm pregnant, and the man who got me this way wants nothing to do with me! I am such a fool, such a stupid fool, for loving him. My life is over. I just want to die. Now, let me finish this, will you?"

"It's not yer time, Miss."

"What do you mean? What could you possibly mean by that?"

"Oh, I'm not getting all mystical on ye," he said. "I'm a good Catholic man, you understand, and my pastor, Father Mike O'Malley, wouldn't understand me talking like this. However, I've been an officer of the law for nigh onto 30 years, and a man sees a lot in that time. I think I know when someone is on their way out, when the spirits have made a place for them, if ye know what I mean. And I don't get that feeling about ye. I don't think they've got the door open yet."

Rosie wanted to scream, she was so frustrated with him. "Listen to yourself! Nothing you say makes sense."

"Well, nobody ever told me making sense was part of me job," he said. "It's hard enough catching criminals and protecting the innocent like yerself, without worrying about making sense of it all."

He was beaming up at her, his absurd face somehow looking like a baby in spite of his white hair and wrinkles. When he winked at her, she couldn't help but smile.

"You're the most nonsensical policeman I've ever met," she said, throwing her hands up. "And yet, somehow you have me believing you. Come on, help me down, dammit. There's someone I need to go see."

"That's me girl!" the policeman said, helping her down. "It's a wise decision yer making."

CHAPTER FIFTEEN

August 7, 1945

Paul sat at his usual booth at Jane's, the dilapidated little waterfront restaurant where he ate most of his meals. He was glad for the break after a morning driving the delivery truck.

"What'll it be for lunch?" said Maggie, the ancient waitress with the gray hair piled on top of her head.

"Coffee, as hot as possible," Paul said. "And how about some of that meatloaf and mashed potatoes? I need something solid today."

Maggie went off to fill the order and Paul turned his head toward the breeze from the upright fan that sat next to the jukebox a few feet away from him. The truck he drove was hot and stank of diesel fuel, and he was hoping the air would clear his head and get rid of the nausea he felt.

He opened the newspaper he'd bought at the newsstand across the street, and the headline: "Atom Bomb Loosed On Hiroshima". He read in wonder about the massive destruction of this new bomb, the way it incinerated whole sections of the Japanese city. Things will never be the same, he thought. Things are speeding up. I hope I can just hang on.

He had reason to hang on. He knew he was lucky to have a job in the first place. With all the servicemen coming back after the end of the war in Europe hungry to find work, jobs were at a premium, and there was little chance an ex-con like him would get hired for anything. It was only through the charity of one of his former customers, a man named Jerry Rosen, that he found anything at all. Rosen saw him when he came in to apply for the job as a driver at Premium Printing, recognized him from his days as the president of Duncan Paper, and he pulled the shipping manager aside and told the man to hire him.

It was a job, and he was grateful for it. The pay allowed him to get a little apartment near the river, and he was slowly getting his life back together. He knew it would never be the same as before; he learned that lesson the first few days after he got out of prison, when he called up some of his old friends from the country club, and none of them would take his calls. They wouldn't have anything to do with him, in spite of the fact that they'd been to his house for years for dinners, had played golf with him, had drunk his liquor. He was a nonperson to them now, he didn't exist anymore. He had broken the rules by getting himself sent to prison; they couldn't contaminate themselves by being seen with him.

Maggie brought the coffee first and he drank deeply, letting the warmth of it penetrate to his bones. He knew his old life was gone, but surprisingly, he didn't miss it all that much. He was grateful for simple things now: for the little apartment, for the freedom he had after the monotony of prison, and most of all for the fact that Lucy hadn't completely ripped him out of her life.

She was letting him back grudgingly, just a little at a time, and he was grateful for that. He would call her once a week, and he'd been to visit her once a month since he got out of prison three months ago. She was still hurt, angry, bitter, but she was at least talking to him.

He could not say that for the children. Oh, Billy was okay, he never talked much anyway. He shrugged at Paul and talked in monosyllables, like most teenage boys. He seemed more interested in joining the Navy and getting out of the house than anything else. He had already enlisted and was due to go to Basic Training in a month. Lucy was worried about him joining the service, but now that the war was almost over her fears were allayed a bit.

Rosie was the real problem. She had been a problem for Lucy the whole time Paul had been in prison, and she had grown into a wild, reckless, headstrong nineteen-year-old girl who smoked cigarettes and drank and went out to nightclubs, where she sang with dance bands.

Part of the reason that Lucy seemed willing to at least talk to Paul was that she was obviously overwhelmed by Rosie and needed to talk to someone about how to raise her. "I worry that she's going to end up dead in a gutter somewhere," she told Paul. "She won't listen to reason when I talk to her. Half the time I don't know where she is, and I don't like the men she's spending time with."

Paul knew Rosie had always been a bit wild. She had been a smart, precocious little girl, but had an odd way of tilting her head and looking at you, like she was looking past you at someone else, or listening to some music only she heard. He hadn't seen her in person since he got out of prison, but he'd seen her high school graduation picture and it showed a black-haired girl with wide blue eyes and a smile that proclaimed she was a free spirit.

She looked a lot like her grandfather Peter Morley, the old scoundrel. Paul had had a lot of time to think in prison, and much of the time his thoughts returned to the man who'd died on his porch twelve years ago, the man who'd walked out of his life so many years before that, the man with the voice that could bring grown men to tears and yet when you looked for him he wasn't there.

Who was he? He never spoke about his childhood, or his past. He was distant even when he was close by. He changed his name, threw off identities like they were old jackets. He could light up a room with his big voice and his laughter, and people wanted to draw near to him, but when you did he was gone -- vanished like a shooting star that flickers across the sky in the blink of an eye. He kept moving, as if he was afraid of what would happen if he stood still for too long.

Maggie brought the rest of his meal, and as Paul dipped his spoon into the mashed potatoes he was suddenly flooded with memories. The smell brought back a time when he was a boy and his father had taken him and his brothers to the saloon where he sang his Irish songs, and the old man had ordered baked potatoes for them. They had sat with their feet dangling from high stools at the bar, with the smell of beer and sawdust and cigar smoke all around them, and they'd happily dug into their potatoes, glad to be in this place of men with their father. Their father was in his element, laughing and joking with the other men, telling stories and bawdy limericks, and singing snatches of songs, attracting men to the brightness and heat that radiated out from him.

It was a brief, happy afternoon and there were few like it in Paul's memory.

It pained him to realize that for all the heartache he'd suffered as a boy because of his father's leaving, he had done something similar to his own children. He'd left them years ago because of his preoccupation with work, with money and success. He had never done the things with them that a father should do with his children; he was absent even when he was present.

And then he'd been truly absent, when he was in prison. He was away for five years, five crucial years when Billy and Rosie needed him the most. He was gone, a cipher in their lives.

How could I have been such a fool? he asked himself. I was abandoned by my own father, and then I did the same thing to my children. That realization hurt more than anything else, more than the shame and humiliation he'd been through in the last five years, more than losing his money and his reputation, more than anything.

"Dad, is that you?"

He looked up to see a young woman standing in front of him, and he realized with a shock it was Rosie. She looked very stylish in a tailored maroon coat with a double row of gold buttons down the front of it, a wide brimmed black hat, and black leather gloves. Her lips were painted bright red. Her face was a bit rounder and more womanly, but otherwise her eyes sparkled just as blue as they had when she was six years old.

She was beautiful, and he was speechless with wonder at this person in front of him.

"May I sit down?" she said.

He was so stunned that he did not react at first, until she raised an eyebrow, and then he got up clumsily and said, "Of course. Yes. Please. Sit down."

He waited till she slid into the booth and then took his seat again. He was so entranced by her that he could not speak at first. She smiled again, and when he realized he was staring dumbly at her, he said, "I'm sorry. It's just, this is such a surprise. I haven't seen you in so long. How did you find me?"

"Mother told me where you worked. I went across the street looking for you, and they said you usually eat your lunch here. Do you mind if I smoke?" She pulled a cigarette out of a long gold case, and put it between her lips. She poised with a lighter in her other hand.

"No, go ahead," he said.

She lit the cigarette, took a drag, and then exhaled a long stream of smoke. She stared out the window at the barges passing by on the river.

"This is near where your company was, right?" she said.

"Not far," he said. "It was about a mile away. You can't see the building from this angle, but you can see it from the parking lot outside. I like to come here because I like being near the river."

"Yes," she said. "It's peaceful here."

"It's great to see you, Rosie," he said. "Your mother has told me a lot about you, and I was hoping I'd see you sometime."

Rosie rolled her eyes. "I bet she's told you plenty about me. We don't get along very well. Has she told you that?"

"Yes," Paul said. "She has. She thinks you're leading a reckless life. She wishes you would be home more. She doesn't understand you."

"Did she tell you I have a job?" Rosie said. "I work nights at a club downtown. I told them I was 21, and they believed me. I make money, and I give Mother some of it for my room and board. It helps her out, and she should be grateful."

"That doesn't sound like a very respectable job," Paul said. "What do you do?"

"Oh, Dad," Rosie said. "You sound just like her. There's nothing wrong with what I'm doing. I started out as a hat-check girl, but I've done pretty much everything. I'm a barmaid, a cigarette girl, and sometimes I get to sing with the bands that come through. I have a good voice, you know. People think I sound like Peggy Lee."

"I remember you always liked to sing," Paul said. "And you had a voice like an angel."

"Singing makes me happy," she said, and she got that faraway look again, the one that she'd had as a child. "I feel like I'm in another world when I'm singing."

"I know it's something special to you," Paul said, measuring his words carefully. "But that's no life for a lady, singing in bars. It's what your grandfather used to do, and he never made much money at it."

"I'm not doing it for the money," Rosie snapped. "I just love to sing, don't you understand that? I have music running through my head all the time. I hear it at the oddest times, just at the edge of my hearing. Sometimes I'll ask other people if they hear it, but nobody ever does. I just have to sing; I would do it even if nobody paid me for it."

"Well, forget about the money," he said, taking a different tack. "That's not the important thing. I just don't think it's a good way to find a husband. You won't find many good men in those places. Not someone you'd want to marry and spend your life with, anyway. Getting married and raising a family are the biggest things you should be thinking about."

She smiled sardonically. "That's rich, coming from you. You didn't set a very good example in that department, did you?"

Paul winced. "You're right, I didn't set a good example. I made a lot of mistakes, and I'll regret them to the end of my days. I wish I could go back in Time and correct what I did wrong, but it's not possible. The only thing I want now is to get back together with your mother. I don't know if it will ever happen, but I think about it all the time. I made such a mess of things." He didn't want to break down, so he paused while he brought himself under control.

"I just don't want to see you make the same mistakes as me." He reached out and took her hand. "Listen," he continued, a sense of urgency in his voice. "We've all been given a free pass. We just went through a war, but our family survived. I made some mistakes and I'm paying for them, but the important thing is we're all alive. We have another chance. Don't you feel it in the air? All these servicemen who will be coming back, they'll have a sense that a new day is dawning. They'll be hungry to grab everything good about life, to get their lives going again. You watch and see, they'll do great things now. I remember being a young man and having those feelings when I came back from the last world war. You feel like you dodged a bullet, and you want to make the most of every minute that's been granted to you."

Rosie looked out the window at the river. The noonday sun had turned it molten gold against a hazy blue sky. "I know," she said. "I can feel it too. I used to work at a USO club and I'd meet men there who were glad to be alive. They wanted to enjoy every minute, you know? They weren't living in the past or future, only the present. I fell in love with one of them."

She paused, exhaling smoke and looking out the window. "He seemed so full of life, so anxious to live every moment, so grateful for everything. He was a British naval officer, and he was sent here with his ship. It was getting repaired at the shipyard. He'd seen a lot of bloodshed, been on two ships that were sunk, and he was just trying to pull himself together. He came to see me at the USO. I was fascinated by him, and I talked to him between sets, and then we started going out. I was mad about him."

Paul's insides were roiling. She was his daughter, after all, and she was only 19. He felt protective toward her, even though she was clearly a woman now. He somehow knew that there was sadness behind her happy story, a bad ending coming. And yet, he was very familiar with what she was experiencing.

"I remember the beginning with your mother," he said, smiling. "I wanted to be with her all the time. I used to make excuses to go see her in the office at the paper mill. Her father didn't like it at all. He was not happy to see this skinny Irish kid mooning around over his daughter. I couldn't stay away, though -- you can't when you're so much in love."

"It's magical, isn't it?" Rosie said, grinning. "You feel like you'll never sleep or eat again. Your whole world has been turned upside down. We had so many dreams and plans. We were going to do so much. He was going to stay in the Navy and we were going to travel around to all his assignments, live all over the world, and I would find singing jobs wherever we were. It was going to be such a dream of a life."

Paul noticed a teardrop in the corner of her eye.

"What happened?" he said, putting his hand out and closing it over hers.

"Everything changed," she said. "It's all so different now. I'm carrying his baby."

"You're what?"

She began to cry, sobbing into her fist, as if she didn't want anyone to hear her. "I'm pregnant," she said. "I don't know, it just happened. I know it's not right, but we couldn't keep our hands off each other. He told me he loved me, we had a special love for each other. Now, he's gone."

Paul ached to hold her in his arms and comfort her the way he did when she was a little girl and something bad happened, like when her favorite dog ran away. He did not know how much she wanted his comfort, did not know if he still had the right to do that after all the mistakes he'd made. So, he did all he could do: he patted her hand over and over.

"It will be all right," he said. "Don't worry, it will be all right."

"No it won't," she said, harshly. "It won't be all right. He didn't want anything to do with me after I told him what happened. He has a wife and son back in London. I was just a wartime fling to him."

Paul was stunned. "What did you say?"

"He's married. He has a wife and a little boy in England. He never told me. I guess he thought he didn't have to. I wasn't that important, in the long run."

In the distance, there was the hoarse grunt of a tugboat's horn.

"Have you told your mother?" Paul said.

Rosie looked at him like he had gone insane. "Are you kidding? She would be furious with me. After all she's been through, I wouldn't do this to her. It might kill her. No, Dad, I came here because I need your support. I have nowhere else to turn. I'm going to get an abortion, and I need money for it."

"Rosie, don't do that."

"Why not? There's no place for this baby. I can't raise it, and you and Mother can barely handle your own lives. You certainly can't handle this. What else can I do?"

He didn't know where the words came from, but somehow they were there: "You can welcome that baby into our family, Rosie. Anytime there's a new soul coming into the family, that's a wondrous, beautiful thing. Why, that's the best news I've heard in years! Don't worry about a thing: your mother and I will take care of it. We'll give that baby a proper family, a loving family. Just think, a new baby! I could get up and dance right here, Rosie."

He gripped her hand so hard she flinched, and he said, "Oh, I'm sorry. . . I'm just so excited. I didn't hurt you, did I?"

She looked at him and shook her head sadly. "You're living in a dream, Dad. Mother won't go for this idea. She barely tolerates you now, and she's only allowing you to see her every couple of weeks. How can you possibly think that she'll let you move back with her and take care of my baby?"

"Because there are things that are stronger than anger," he said, tears filling his eyes. "Love is one of them. I know your mother, and the presence of a baby will soften her heart. I believe the joy and wonder that baby will bring into our family will heal this wound I inflicted on her. You'll see, Rosie. It will happen."

She pushed his hand away. "I don't know why I should believe anything you say. You broke your marriage vow, Dad. That was worse than anything else you did. I saw you kissing that blonde German lady when I was just a kid. I never looked at you the same after that. You lied to all of us, and I can't believe anything you say now. What's to stop you from running off with someone else?"

The whistle went off that signaled the end of the lunch break at the printing plant across the street. Men were getting up from their seats and paying their bills so they could get back to work. Paul could hear the ticking of the clock on the wall, and he was aware that this was a moment when he had to rise to the occasion, step up and be the father he had not been before.

"You need to go back to work, right?" Rosie said. "I'll leave now. If you won't help me, I'll find some other way to get the money I need." She started to get up.

"No!" Paul grabbed her arm, clutching her like a drowning man grabbing an oar held out to him from a life raft. "Don't do it. Please. I know you have no reason to trust me, but I promise I'll be there for you. Please, Rosie. We can be a family again, I am sure of it. Let me talk to Lucy; I know she'll be with me on this. We'll welcome that baby into our family, and we'll bring it up with love."

"You'll be the talk of the town," Rosie snapped. "Don't you realize that? Your tramp of a daughter got herself pregnant, and you're bringing up the baby? What a story that will be. You won't be able to show your faces anywhere."

Paul smiled. "We can't worry about that now, Rosie. I was in prison, remember? I bankrupted my company and made speeches for a pro-German organization. I'm already a scandal. Besides, I lived through this a long time ago, when I was a boy. My mother was shunned by all the 'respectable' Irish in West Philadelphia because her husband left her. My brothers and I got into a lot of fights in the schoolyard because of that. I have a thick skin by now; I can handle it.

"Besides, none of that really matters," he continued. "What matters is that there is a baby coming, and we should make a place for it in our hearts. Life continues, and we have to do our best to make it flower. Why, we have no idea what this baby will do in its life! It could do amazing, wonderful things, Rosie! Please. Let me talk to your mother. I'll make it work."

Rosie's body relaxed for just a split second, as if she wanted to put her head down and weep. She looked like she was carrying the weight of the world on her shoulders and she wanted someone to lean on, even if for only a moment. She sat back in the booth, closed her eyes, and said, "Okay, Dad. I'll do what you say. I hope it's the right decision."

"It is," he said, squeezing her hand. "You wait and see what it's like to have this baby come into your life. You just wait."

CHAPTER SIXTEEN

December 18, 1947

Edith knew there was something familiar about the man as soon as she saw him. It was close to dinnertime when he came in to the store, holding the hand of a little tousle-haired boy who seemed ecstatically happy that he was going to have a dish of ice cream. They sat at the counter and Edith gave them two silver bowls of chocolate ice cream, and it touched her to see the joy on the man's face as he watched the little boy eat. He acted more like a playmate than a grandfather, which is what she guessed he was.

"Your mother won't be happy about this, Pete," the man said to the little boy. "I expect she'll be cross with me for feeding you ice cream at this late hour. We won't tell her, though, will we?" he said, winking at Edith behind the counter.

It was the man's voice that gave him away. Edith had heard that ringing bell of a voice before. It was a beautiful speaking voice, and she remembered the last time she'd heard it -- in 1939 in the Athenaeum auditorium, when he was warming the audience up for the speech by that Nazi sympathizer Hans Guenther.

It was Paul Morley, son of the man she had been married to so many years before. The Paul Morley who'd been associated with a right wing organization that had been linked to the Nazi party. The man who'd been there when Simon almost got killed in the riot at the back of the hall.

But all that was so long ago, before the war. So many things had happened since then. Morley had been to prison, she knew from reading the newspapers. Guenther had disappeared, and then turned up in Germany during the war and was killed, but not before he and his kind had put in motion the machinery that slaughtered so many millions of innocent people.

Including her brother Edward, who'd died one night during the bombing of London. He was an air raid warden and he'd been killed trying to help a family get out of their burning home, when it collapsed on him. Edith had read the news in a telegram from her Aunt Eunice. Edward had two children, both boys that she hadn't seen since they were babies. Eunice said one of them had disappeared and the other had died of malaria in India, where he'd been posted in the Army during the 1930s.

And the war had reached its ugly claws over here, too, and taken one of her family. Her son John had been killed in 1943 at an explosion at the Navy Yard, where he was working on a destroyer that had come in for repairs.

Now there was only Mercy, and she was an uncertain presence in Edith's life, never really there even when she was there. She had moved to Detroit last year after her most recent marriage broke up, and in the last letter Edith had received from her she said she was working in a plant that manufactured tanks.

It got Edith angry to think about all the damage brought about by that ugly Nazi regime. She looked at Paul Morley and she wanted to slap him across the face for his role in it. But then she saw the tender way that he treated the little boy, the simple joy he had in the presence of this young life, and her heart softened. What would the point be? she thought. The war is over, and he seems like he was punished for his crime.

She remembered reading in the newspapers that he'd been sent off to prison for embezzlement. He'd been chastened, she could read that in his lined and careworn face. Yes, he had been an instrument of evil in the world, a person who'd fanned the flames of hatred and murderous rage, but she could see that he was not the same man as he had been in 1939. He had the same voice, but his face was deeply lined and his hair had turned white. The blue eyes shining out from his ruined face looked wounded, and he seemed like a man whose life had fallen apart.

Let it go, Edith, she told herself. He has paid some kind of price for what he did, that is obvious. Don't say a word; just let him live his life in whatever peace he can find now.

When the man and his grandson finished their ice cream and he stood up to pay, she could not resist, however. "Don't I know you?" she said. "You look very familiar."

An emotion like shame passed over his face, and he looked away for a moment. "I don't know," he said. "Ah, you might have seen my picture in the paper."

"No, I think it was something else," she said. "We met before. . .at the funeral of your father. . . my husband. I am Edith Francis."

He looked relieved, probably because she wasn't referring to his criminal past. "Oh, yes, now I remember. That was in 1935. Seems a long time ago now, doesn't it?"

"How are you?" she said.

"Oh, I'm surviving," he said. He had picked the little boy up and had him in his arms. "This little fellow helps me put things in perspective. My grandson Pete."

"How do you do?" Edith said. The little boy smiled at her, and she could see the same light in his eyes that his grandfather James had. Suddenly she felt the need to tell Paul something. He might never come back in this store, she realized, so she might never have this opportunity again.

"Would it be possible for you stop back later?" she said. "I have something I would like to show you. It has to do with your father."

A range of emotions flickered across his face: anger, hurt, sadness, bitterness. He finally got control of himself, though, and said: "Why, yes, Edith -- it is Edith, isn't it? I only live about ten blocks away. I'll just take little Pete home, because it's past his suppertime, then I'll stop back."

"I close the store at 9:00 every evening," she said. "That would be a good time to come back."

"Good. I'll see you then." Paul shifted the little boy in his arms, the boy waved goodbye, and they went out into the night.

When they left Edith went upstairs to the little apartment over the store where she lived now, and she went to her dresser and got out the jewelry box from the top drawer. She unlocked it with a small key she kept under her pillow, and opened the carved, polished wood box and took out an envelope. In large bold letters it said, "To Edith Francis". She put the letter in the pocket of her sweater and then went back downstairs.

At ten minutes to 9 the door opened and Paul walked in the store. Edith was waiting on a boy and girl, teenagers who had come in for ice cream sodas, and Paul sat at the counter and ordered a root beer. He made small talk with her till the couple got up and paid their bill and she let them out of the store, locking the door behind them.

She came over and sat next to Paul at the counter.

"I'll get right to the point," she said. "I have something to show you that I think you should read." She took the envelope out of her pocket. "Here," she said, handing it over to him without any ceremony. "You'll want to read this."

He looked puzzled, but he opened the envelope, took out the letter inside, and began to read. There were small knots of muscles in his jaw that moved as he read, and his face slowly turned pink with emotion. His hand shook as he got further along in the letter, and Edith thought she could see a single small tear forming at the edge of one eye.

It was a two-page letter, written on both sides of the paper, and when he finished one sheet he put it down on the counter carefully and started the second one. He did not speak until he finished, and the only sound was the big round Coca Cola clock ticking on the wall.

When he got to the end, he put his hand over his face for a moment, to compose himself, then turned to Edith.

"This is the letter I found on him when he died, right?"

"Yes," she said. "It was addressed to me, but I've often thought you should read it. I didn't know when I'd ever see you again, and I thought there's no time like the present."

He sighed deeply, letting his whole body go limp.

"Would you like some tea?" Edith said. "I have a pot on. Perhaps that would help."

"Thank you," he said. "I would like a cup of tea."

She got the blue porcelain teapot from the counter and poured two cups of tea, one for herself and one for him. She gave him a saucer with sugar cubes in it, and he put two in his cup and stirred it, then took a drink.

"I remember my father drinking tea at home," Paul said, finally. "He would spend Sundays, his day off from his chauffeur job, with us, and he drank tea all day long. He would get very irritated if my mother ran out of tea."

"That was the Irish in him," Edith said. "They are great tea drinkers, like the English. I can't live without my tea."

"I am glad you showed me this letter," Paul said. "It explains some things about him. I was very angry at him for most of my life."

"I think it must have been difficult for him to live with such a terrible secret," Edith said. "He was just a boy and he killed a man. He had to leave his home because of it, and come across the sea to this big, alien country. I don't think he ever got over it."

"You know, I do have some good memories of him," Paul said. "My brother Tim and I would wait up for him when he came home from singing at the saloon on Saturday nights. He came in smelling of cigar smoke, beer, and peanuts. He was always in a happy mood, and just the sound of his voice would make me glad. I'd scramble out of bed at 2 in the morning just to put my arms around him and sit on his lap and listen to the stories he'd tell. My mother would scold him for keeping us up so late, but he'd always make her laugh with some joke, and we knew things would be all right. When he was happy he could make you feel like everything was right with the world; when he got in one of his black moods, it was like you found out there was a cruel joke at the bottom of your life."

"I know," Edith said, sipping her tea. "He made our children feel the same way. They were crazy about him. That's why it hurt them so badly when they found out he betrayed me. They never recovered, really."

"He hurt a lot of people, that's for sure," Paul said. "My brother Tim couldn't handle it. I guess I just tried all the harder to get along without a father, to make my way in the world. It was important to me to be a success, to make up for the hole my father left in my life."

"We all muddle along, don't we?" Edith said. "We fumble and fall down and make our way somehow."

"Well, he made a lot of mistakes, but then we all do," Paul said. "I've certainly made my share."

"It's part of life," Edith said. "What's sad is to live your life and die feeling that you're unforgiven, like your father must have."

Paul blinked, put his hand up to his face again, and his eyes filled with tears. "Well, that's me, for sure. These days, when I read the reports in the newspapers of the concentration camps, I feel like I am filthy with guilt for my part in all that, in promoting that ugly philosophy. I don't know what possessed me to get involved with that Guenther man. Ego, I guess. And I lost my head over that wife of his. I regret so much. I made speeches that I wish with all my heart I could take back. I feel responsible in some way for spreading hate. Stupid, stupid, stupid. God, it's a horrible thing I did, and I can't believe I'll ever be forgiven for it."

She put her hand out and touched his arm. "You will be. You are. God forgives you."

He shook his head. "No. I don't feel that way. My wife, my children. . ."

"They will forgive you," she said. "It's the only way to break the spell of anger and hate. And there is always hope. You have that grandson, don't you? He should give you so much hope for the future."

His face brightened. "Yes, he's a happy little fellow. I look at him and my heart lifts. He doesn't know evil. Every day he wakes up and it's a brand new world. He looks for goodness, for reasons to smile."

"Treasure that feeling," she said. "It will keep you in the light."

He smiled, gratitude in his eyes. "Thank you," he said. "I will. And what about you? Do you have something to give you hope? Grandchildren, maybe?"

She sighed. "I don't have any grandchildren. My son was killed during the war in an explosion at the Navy Yard, where he worked. My daughter Mercy has no children. I am not without hope, though." Her eyes twinkled. "God smiled on me in my heartache, after James, er, your father, died. I got a job here at this little store, and I got to know the owner, a wonderful man named Simon Levin. He and I spent many happy hours together. I loved him, though in a different way than I loved your father. When the war came it was very wrenching for him, because he had relatives in Germany and he was afraid for them."

Paul looked down, ashamed. "It was people like me who helped that madness along."

She touched his arm. "You made a bad mistake. You have repented of it, I am sure. If we can't forgive ourselves, the world will never get any better, will it? Anyway, there was a miracle of miracles. Most of Simon's family survived the war. Some of them managed to get out before it started, and others were hidden by decent, God-fearing men and women over there. A few survived the camps. A few died, but fewer than he expected, much less than most families lost. It was a miracle, to be sure.

"Where is he now?" Paul said. "Did you marry him?"

"He moved to Palestine with many of his relatives. They want to start fresh, in the new country of Israel. So you see, hope blooms anew."

Paul frowned. "But what about you? You love this man, right? Has he abandoned you?"

"Oh, Heavens, no," she said, laughing. "I am going to join him there in a couple of months. I stayed behind to sell the store for him, and to clean up the paperwork. We are going to be married when I get there. I'm 70 years old and he's 74, but I don't suppose that's too old to start a new life, do you?"

"No, not at all," Paul said. "You know as well as me, my father started many new lives. Age never stopped him."

"That's right," Edith said. "But, Paul, there is one thing I would like to do before I leave."

"What's that?"

"I would like to show that letter to your mother, if she's still alive. Is she?"

Paul smiled. "Yes. She's 85 years old, God bless her. Still as stubborn as ever, though. I wanted her to come and live with me, but she won't do it. The man she married after my father left, Martin Lancaster, died a few years ago, so she was living all alone. She was getting too old to live on her own, so I arranged for her to move into a home run by nuns in West Philadelphia."

"Do you think she would mind a visit from me?"

Paul thought about it for a moment. "There was a time when she probably would not have wanted to see you, but that's long past. She had another love in her life since my father left. Martin Lancaster was a prince of a man, and she loved him very much. I don't think she would mind a visit from you. And if you let her read the letter, it might clear some things up for her, like it did for me."

"Then I'll go," Edith said. "I would dearly love to see Rose again."

CHAPTER SEVENTEEN

January 22, 1948

Rose shuffled down the tiled corridor and made her way to the chapel. Morning Mass was over, and she liked to sit in the chapel for awhile around 11:00 before it was time to join the other old people in the dining room for lunch.

She pushed open the door to the chapel and went in, and immediately felt more peaceful amid the glow from the candles in front of the shrine to Mary on the side.

It is strange, she thought, easing into a pew in front of the altar, how I've ended up here, of all places. There were years when a Catholic church was the last place I wanted to be.

She had thought she would end her life in St. Paul's Episcopal church, the granite faced church on 23rd street near where she and Martin lived. She felt welcomed there, and she knew it was where Martin felt most at home. There were no disapproving looks, no whispers as she walked by the way there had been so many years before in her parish church when she went there with Peter.

But of course, Martin was gone now. She felt the stab of sadness that pierced her heart, the memory that never faded, of how he crossed the street that snowy night five years ago right in front of her, and was hit broadside by a car he never saw, his body flying like some airborne thing for a few seconds, till it landed with a thud on the sidewalk right in front of her feet.

The car screeched to a stop and she saw the door open and the horrified face of the driver, a boy hardly older than a teenager, his eyes like saucers and his mouth opened in a silent scream as he looked at the lifeless body on the sidewalk. She saw, too, how his eyes met hers and with a look of stark terror he slammed the door, floored the gas, and sped off down the street, his tires squealing like a banshee. She imagined that the picture of Martin's body on the sidewalk was etched into his mind the way it was hers.

Poor Martin. He died because he was losing his eyesight, but he was trying to hide it from her. He kept going to work every day pretending nothing was wrong, even though she knew he could barely read anymore, and some days the world was not much more than a blur to him. His clients told her the truth. She had always taken them in, the detritus of the city, people who washed up on the shores of the justice system, and who sometimes had no place to stay. She let them sleep on a cot in the basement, and she cooked meals for them till Martin got their legal problems sorted out, but the last few years they were telling her stories of how he had to get courthouse clerks to read legal documents for him, and how he had almost gotten run over several times already crossing the street in front of City Hall.

She pleaded with him to go to a doctor, but all he said was, "I know what it is. Diabetes runs in my family, and it's because of that. Just a little blurred vision, is all. I can handle it."

He was still working because he was worried that he hadn't made enough money for her to live on. "I don't have much to show for all my years of work," he had said. It was a losing battle, though, because funds were always short for his clients, and most of them couldn't pay him what he should have earned for his time.

But she didn't care about money. She had done without it for so long she had learned to live on the absence of it. She wanted

Martin, nothing more. His quiet presence had been her lifeline for so long, and she did not know how she could live without him. To lose him would be like the very ground under her feet opening up, and she could not conceive of that.

But it happened anyway, and right in front of her eyes. She wailed and raged against God many nights after that, and would have spit in God's eye if she was able to.

Paul and Lucy were a great comfort, now that they were back together, but even though they pleaded with her to move in with them, she would not do it.

"You don't want an old woman like me cluttering up your house," she said. "The world is full of promise, now that the war is over. You have youth in your house, a baby, with so much appetite for life. You don't need me putting a damper on things with all my aches and pains."

No, she would not do that. She stayed in her own house, but within a year that became impractical. She was having what she called "spells" where she would get lightheaded and fall down, and several times her neighbors found her on the floor unconscious. Paul was worried about her, and he finally said that if she wouldn't move in with him and Lucy he was going to find a place for her in an old person's home.

That was how she ended up here, in the Little Sisters of the Poor home. It was a plain brick building in West Philadelphia, with rooms that were Spartan in their simplicity. A bed and a cheap wooden dresser, a chair and a table with a crucifix on the wall. A few hooks to hang your clothes on. Not that she had a lot of clothing. Rose had dispensed with most of her possessions when she moved in here. She didn't need all that clutter in her life; she wanted to be free of it.

The life was a simple one, punctuated by routine. Besides three meals a day, there was Mass in the morning and benediction in the late afternoon. The sisters moved among them like smiling, silent angels, in their black habits with gray headdresses and white bands around their foreheads. They seemed happy in their work, and their good humor and humility warmed Rose's heart. None of them judged her in any way, and she felt loved and cared for to such a degree that she was content for the first time in years. It astonished Paul when he came to visit. For a long time he seemed unable to believe it. "You're quite sure you don't want to come live with Lucy and me?" he would say. "You'd have a bedroom that's three times the size of this. The food would be better. You can't tell me you'd rather stay here."

But she did. There was something comforting about the place. She had a few friends, women who had been domestic servants like herself, who told stories of the grand houses they had worked in and the prominent families they had lived with for many years. They had all come over from places like Ireland or Scotland when they were girls, just as Rose had, and none of them had been back to their homelands. Most said their families were all gone now, just like Rose's.

It was nice to have companions like this, but what Rose liked most was to sit here in the chapel, in front of the Immaculate Heart of Mary altar. Mary had become important to her now, because she was a mother who had her heart pierced by this cruel world, and Rose could understand that. The statue was of a girl who looked as old as Rose was when she had come to America, a woman robed in blue and white, with her red heart pierced with a band of thorns. At first Rose had been attracted to the statue because that heart looked like the way her own wounded heart felt, but now she simply gazed into those eyes, which seemed to offer such comfort and love.

Her reverie was interrupted by a tap on the shoulder, and she looked up to see Sister Rita, a young Italian nun with merry black eyes, who whispered, "Mrs. Morley, there is someone here to see you."

Rose was shocked, because she never got visitors, besides Paul and his family. She had no idea who it could be, and in fact she thought of telling the Sister that it must be a mistake. However, the nun seemed so convinced, even putting a hand under her elbow to help her up, and so she went along, her head full of questions.

The nun led her out to the large sitting room outside the dining area. There were couches and overstuffed chairs there, and Rose saw a face she recognized, and a small, compact body that rose to greet her. It was Edith, the woman Peter had left her for.

She was older of course, but she still had her trim little body and her precise, dancer's carriage. Her hair had turned gray, arranged in a neat little helmet on her head, but otherwise she looked not much changed.

"Hello, Rose," she said, taking Rose by the hand. "I don't suppose you remember me? We met at the funeral of my, ah, husband. I am Edith Francis."

"Of course I remember you," Rose said, sitting down across from her in a big upholstered chair. "I am surprised to see you."

"Yes, I am sure you are. I will tell you why I am here in a moment, but first, how are you?"

"I am as well as can be expected," Rose said. "I am 86 years old, after all. I have aches and pains, and I spend a lot of my time thinking about things that happened in my childhood, but other than that I am doing well. Now, what brings you here?"

"I have wanted to speak with you for many years," Edith said. "I was quite upset the last time we met, at the funeral of my, ah, husband, and I left in a hurry. I have often wanted to meet with you again and talk, but I did not know how to get in touch with you."

"How did you find me?" Rose said.

"It is a strange thing," the other woman said. "I have been employed at a little store on Market street, a little corner store with a soda fountain in it, and not long ago your son Paul came in, with his grandson.

"He looked familiar to me," she continued. "Both he and the boy had a look about them that reminded me of my, ah, husband."

"Aye," Rose said. "That little fellow looks a lot like Peter Morley."

"He does, quite a bit," Edith said. "Although I see him as resembling my James Francis." She smiled, abashed. "The man was a chameleon, it seemed, and I suppose he had other names too."

Rose remembered the boy Sean McCarthy, so tall and bold back in Skibbereen. "That he did. When I first met him he was calling himself Sean McCarthy."

Edith shook her head. "I used to despair of ever knowing him," she said. "He was a man who loved to talk, but in spite of that he never revealed much about himself."

"Well I know it," Rose said. "I know nothing about his life before I met him, and yet I lived in close quarters with him for 20 years and had three children with him."

"He would not talk about the past," Edith said. "He would say, 'My life began when I met you, darling,' and try to charm me out of asking questions. I just thought he was a very private man, although it always bothered me. Then, when I found out that he had been, ah, married before. . . I thought that was the big secret he had been hiding."

"I don't think there was one secret with that man," Rose said. "There were many."

"Yes," Edith said. "And that is why I came to see you. There is a secret I feel you should know about him."

"A secret?" Rose said. "Why do I need to know anything more about the man? It has been 15 years since he died. It's well past time for me to be worrying about secrets that Peter Morley had."

Edith hesitated, her eyes welling up. "It mattered to me when I found it out. Your son Paul came in 1935 to tell me that Peter, ah, James had died at his house. He found a letter in James's pocket, addressed to me. It told the most extraordinary story."

Her voice faltered, and she turned her head away. Rose reached over and patted her on the arm, and she took a deep breath and went on.

"The letter said that when he was a young man in Ireland, he killed a man," Edith said. "With his bare hands."

"What?" Rose said. "Are you serious? I don't believe it. Peter, or James, or whatever he went by in those days, I don't think he had it in him. For all his faults, he was not a violent man. I can't see him doing something like that."

"The man he killed was a British soldier," Edith said. "An officer. James said the officer was harassing him about something, some petty crime or other, and something in him just snapped. He beat the officer to death."

"When did this happen?" Rose said. She was still astonished, and could hardly believe her ears.

"I don't know the year," Edith said. "He was 20, I think. He said he woke up every morning of his life thinking of it, and dreamed of it at night. It's why he left Ireland. It's why he was always changing his name, creating new identities."

It was true, Rose suddenly realized. She did not want to believe it, but something inside her told her it was true. It explained so many things about this boy she met in Ireland, and the mysterious man he became. It explained the sadness behind the laughter, the hole that was always there, the gulf between him and other people, the blackness that came over him even in the midst of his happiest moods.

"You say my son Paul gave this letter to you?" Rose said. "Paul never mentioned it to me."

"He never opened the letter," Edith said, "so he never knew the story. I only met your son that one time, when James died. Then recently when he came to the store, I recognized him and we got to talking, and I ended up showing him the letter. He seemed deeply moved, and it was then that I got the notion to show the letter to you. He told me where you lived, and that is why I am here."

"I am amazed that Paul even read the letter," Rose said. "He never wanted anything to do with his father. He has a lot of bitterness because of what happened."

"We all have bitterness," Edith said, her eyes filling up again. "I still have it, although I also have compassion for James for what he went through. I understand him more than I ever did years ago. He was carrying a great burden, but no one knew that. I wanted you to know."

Rose sighed. It was all so long ago, and she had put it out of her mind, but now it came rushing back. The feelings, the ache of it all, the terrible loneliness that came with loving this man, it all came back now like water breaking through a dam. She still loved him, after all, even though she also loved Martin with all her heart and soul. But there was something about a first love that could not be denied. Once you opened your heart to someone, there was always a part that remained attached, a bond that could never be broken.

"I am not sure my son will ever forgive him," Rose said. "He wouldn't allow his father's name to be spoken in his presence."

"My daughter Mercy feels the same way," Edith said. "She loved him so much, and because of that the betrayal hurt her deeply. She has never been able to have a strong relationship with a man, and I think that is the reason."

"He hurt a lot of people," Rose said.

"I know," Edith said. "That is why I came; to give you all some understanding of this man who affected all of our lives." She touched Rose on the wrist. "Maybe this will give us all some peace."

"Maybe you are right," Rose said. "I have one more question, though. Do you know the name of the British officer? Was there a name in the letter?"

"Why yes," Edith said. "It was Charlesworth. Lieutenant Charlesworth."

Rose was thunderstruck. That was the name of the father of Rosie's child.

CHAPTER EIGHTEEN

July 1, 1952

To my dear mother,

If my son Paul knew I was writing this letter to a dead person, he'd surely think I had gone daft. I often suspect he thinks that anyway, for he looks at me sometimes and shakes his head, and will say that he cannot understand me, claiming that I am a "stubborn, willful old woman".

I feel the need to write this, however, because letter writing has always helped me to get my thoughts collected, and it calms me. I know I can never mail this letter to you, but I fancy that you may be able to read it anyway, as perhaps you are looking over my shoulder the way I have felt you do so many times.

Today is my 90th birthday. I feel like I have lived for such a long time. I never expected this; I thought if I were lucky I might live to be 70. You left this earth when you were 60, and there were times after Peter disappeared when I used to wonder if I would make it even that long.

It has been such an eternity since I've seen you in the flesh! I left home when I was 18, and that was 72 years ago. I have no photographs of you, but I can still picture you in my mind just as clear as when I left. I remember how I tried to make you understand that I was leaving, and how you looked at me with those lost and forsaken eyes, the wild joy and the anguish mixed together. I told you I would be back; it is one of the chief sorrows of my life that I did not get back to see you again.

But of course, you have been with me in some way ever since, have you not? I have felt your presence in my life so many times. I have heard the lilt of your soft voice in the breeze on a summer afternoon, and I have heard the sadness of your lullabies in the music of a far off train whistle. I have smelled the basil thyme you gathered in the fields even though I am in the middle of a crowded street in the city, and it comes to me sometimes now when I am alone in my room. I have seen you in the flame of a candle and in the shadows cast by the full moon.

I used to think that I saw and heard and smelled these things because I had a touch of your madness, and I worried for years that I would turn out like you, wandering about with my hair uncombed and my clothing rent, babbling on about spirits and fairies. I think there were times when I got close to it, but I never went over the edge. I always pulled back, because I had children to think of.

What were you trying to tell me all those years? I longed to touch you, to lay my head on your breast again like I did when I was a girl. This world was such a frightening, terrible place at times, and I was always tempted by visions of another world. I wanted to flee from it, back to the world of my childhood -- or at least, the world that you made for us with your stories and songs, the bright illuminated world I remembered.

I never told anyone of this, not even Martin. I kept it all to myself. I thought that this life was one of suffering and toil, and all a person could do was put one foot in front of the other and get on with it.

You beckoned to me and I was afraid to come near, yet I longed so much to see you again. I have often wondered if there truly is another world beyond this one. Were you trying to show it to me? I have had a troubled time with my faith. The Church taught us that there is another world, but it was not our place to think about it yet, while we were on this earth. I used to go into churches and look at the statues of saints, and wonder if they were at all like me, if they thought about such things as I did. Did they see spirits hovering in the air? The priests gave us a pattern for our faith -- the prayers and the devotions, the feast days and the liturgy -- but I never felt at ease with that pattern. I kept wondering if the old stories you told, of ancient myths and fairies and another world, were also true, along with the story of Our Lord and His crucifixion.

Here I am 90 years old, and I still wonder. But, I feel a turning inside me. Perhaps it is because I live in a place run by nuns, and I go to a chapel every day, but now I am more at peace with my spiritual life. I pray to Our Mother Mary, and I feel close to her because she had a wounded heart, like me. Like all mothers. Our hearts are always wounded by the world, aren't they? We feel so much for those people closest to us, and their suffering becomes our suffering. Every wound becomes deeper, harsher, has more of an ache to it. I realize now that Mary suffered a mother's love to an infinite degree, seeing what the world did to her precious Son. I cannot help but be moved by her suffering, her tears, and her agony. She is a model for me, and there are times when I truly think she understands. At times in the chapel she reaches out her hands to me, she comforts me with her tears, and she tells me it will all turn out right in the end.

It has taken away my fear of dying. I always pressed on, just trying to ignore the spirit side of things, because I could not come to terms with it. I was afraid that death would mean oblivion for me and for those I loved. I did not want to think about that, so I put my head down and kept going. In the last few years, though, I have come to feel that there is another world waiting for me, and that I will see all of my loved ones again. I will see you again, Mother, and we will laugh and sing the old songs, and tell the old stories. I will see Peter and Martin and my sons, my darling sons Tim and Willy, who left me so long ago. Our Mother has told me so.

I will put this letter away in the drawer of my dresser, and when I am gone someone will find it and give it to my family. Maybe it will help them, I don't know. It is the story of a woman who lived a long time and saw much, and finally came to some peace about things that were troubling her for so many years.

Goodbye, Mother. I hope you have gained some peace, I hope you have found your other world of fairies and heroes, and you are able to sit under the new moon and watch them dance to their beautiful music.

And maybe in not too long a time I will join you there.

Rose

CHAPTER NINETEEN

November 9, 1960

"Grandmother, have you heard the news? John F. Kennedy won the election!"

Rose opened her eyes and saw the young woman standing next to her. At first she did not recognize her, but that was normal these days. It often took her several minutes to orient herself when she woke up, to place the faces that were peering at her so intently.

"It's me, Rosie," the woman said. "Your granddaughter, remember?"

Rosie. She felt suddenly happier, hearing that name. She remembered the little girl with the black pageboy haircut who would look at her with those soulful blue eyes and speak to her with that air of wisdom beyond her years. She was an intelligent little girl, full of questions but also answers of her own making, full of some wisdom that she seemed to have been born with, prone to making odd statements, laughing at her own little jokes. When she was just a toddler she would laugh and smile and point at something behind Rose, as if there were a person standing there, but Rose would turn around and there was never anyone there. She was different, but she seemed happy with herself, and Rose enjoyed her company immensely.

"What did you say, dear? The Kennedy boy won the election?"

"Yes," Rosie said, clapping her hands. "It's wonderful, isn't it? I rushed right over to tell you. He's the first Catholic President this country has ever had. And his grandparents were born in Ireland."

"It's a miracle, to be sure," Rose said. "A happy day."

"You've lived through so much, grandmother," Rosie said. "Did you ever expect to see this? An Irish Catholic President!"

Rose shook her head. "Why, of course not! When I came here, we didn't think any of us could be the President. I didn't expect to stay anyway. I was just trying to help my family, to keep them from starving to death on the farm. Oh, that's all in the past now. I'd rather talk about you. When are you going to get married?"

Rosie laughed. "Oh, we're back to that, are we? I haven't met the right man, grandmother. I've been too busy getting my singing career off the ground."

"Singing career? I told you before, that's not a proper thing for a woman to do. Wearing those spangled gowns and spending your time in nightclubs. Sometimes I think you've got too much of your grandfather in you. He had a beautiful singing voice too, and look where it got him."

"I only met him once, when I was a little girl," Rosie said. "I wish I had known him better." She got a faraway look in her eyes. "I never heard him sing."

"He had a voice that could touch your soul," Rose said. "He should have been on the stage, but it was not God's plan for that to happen."

She pulled the covers around her peremptorily. "Now listen to me: you have a beautiful voice, Rosie, but life isn't just about singing. You should find someone and settle down. Family is important. I won't be around forever, and I want to see my family settled and getting along with their lives before I leave. That boy of yours needs a father, you know."

Rosie sighed. "I know he does, grandmother, but the kind of men I've been meeting in the entertainment field are not the best fathers. It just hasn't been the best place for meeting someone to marry. Now, before we go into a complete examination of my love life, like so many times in the past, let's talk about something else. Think about it! A son of Erin is in the White House! Things have changed for the better, haven't they?"

"Yes, I suppose so," Rose said. "I'm happy about it, but I have other things on my mind this morning. Help me out of this bed, and take me to the chapel. I want to say some prayers of thanksgiving."

"But grandmother, you know you're not allowed out of bed. The nuns say you can't walk anymore."

"That's nonsense. I am able to walk just fine with the help of my cane, but they don't let me because they'd rather keep me cooped up in this room. It's easier for them, you see. I haven't been to the chapel in ages, and I want to go back. I want to sit in front of Mary and say my prayers."

It took some doing, but eventually Rose convinced her granddaughter to take her to the chapel, although she had to agree to go in a wheelchair. Rosie wheeled her down the hallway, and every time one of those meddlesome nuns stopped to tell her she shouldn't be out of bed, Rose had a few choice words to leave her open-mouthed and staring in shock.

Soon they were in the chapel, and Rose felt herself finally relax. It had been months since she'd been back there; the nuns were worried about her shortness of breath, and her shaky legs, and they had confined her to bed most days.

She motioned for Rosie to push her over to the statue of Mary with the Immaculate Heart. She sat there and looked at the sad eyes, the pierced heart, and the outstretched hands and suddenly she felt a wave of emotion wash over her. Tears filled her eyes and she felt her breath coming in ragged gasps. She saw Rosie kneel by the railing and bow her head in silent prayer, and she tried to do the same.

The chapel was too crowded, though. All of a sudden there were shapes, faces in the flickering half light from the candles. There was her father, her brother Brian, her sisters Theresa and Annie. They were all there, along with other faces from her past. There was Sean McCarthy, singing "Dear Old Skibbereen" with that smile and that glint in his eye. There also was Mary Driscoll, and all of the Lancasters, and Martin, dear Martin, with his kind eyes and his warm, gentle hands, smiling and waving to her.

And there, standing next to them all, was her mother. She was not the wild-eyed woman of her later years, but the spirited red-haired young woman of her youth, who sang the merry songs and laughed with such exuberance it beckoned you to laugh with her.

"Ah, my darling girl," she said, in her singsong voice. "Do you not know that I was only after trying to make you see there's another world, that this one is but the skin on the surface of a deeper realm, and that the suffering we go through is not in vain. The pain, why it doesn't last long, my girl. Think of it as a pause in the middle of a song. We go on to sing the next verse. There is always another verse, you see. There is a deeper world, and this is only a way station for us."

Rose moved her lips, whispering. "Why is there so much pain? Why is there so much heartache? Why do the ones we love have to leave us? Why is a mother's beating heart ripped out of her chest?"

"Look at the Immaculate Heart, Rose. There you will find your answers."

Rose looked and saw the Heart glowing with love, with the eternal love of God, with the passion and love and endless oceans of mercy, the outstretched hands of God, the comfort that salves all wounds. It was an endless wave of emotion, more mercy than she could have ever hoped to be worthy of, and she felt herself trembling with the intensity of it. Her body was tingling, numb, and her head felt full, she felt in the throes of some great wave washing over her, taking her with its power and washing her clean. She tried to call out to Rosie, but the words wouldn't come. She tried to get out of the wheelchair, wanting desperately to walk towards the people she saw, but her limbs wouldn't work.

It was too much, too intense. Her heart was too small, she feared it would break. What was this feeling? Happiness? The ache of sadness? Longing? The joy of her deepest hopes realized? Was she going to see her family again?

She gave one small shudder, then sat back, a wisp of a smile on her face.

Her granddaughter Rosie was suddenly conscious of a deep silence in the chapel. Something was different.

She looked around, wondering what had happened.

She saw her grandmother with her head back, a smile on her lips, and suddenly she knew. The memory of her grandfather lying dead on the porch of her house came back, in vivid colors, and she recognized that look.

"Goodbye, grandmother," she said. "Goodbye."

CHAPTER TWENTY

December 24, 1960

Dear Edith:

I found your address in my mother's papers and I hope you haven't moved, because I pray this letter reaches you.

I wanted to write and tell you that my mother Rose passed away on November 9. She died in the chapel at the home where she lived. It was a peaceful death, and my daughter Rosie was there with her at the time.

We had the funeral a few days later at the cathedral of Saints Peter and Paul in Philadelphia. It is a very fancy high-church kind of place, and my mother rarely attended Mass there, but she had an old friend named Mary Driscoll who was prominent in the local Catholic archdiocese, and she arranged for the funeral Mass to be said at that church. Mary was a good friend of the Cardinal, and it was through her efforts that my mother got such a beautiful service. The cathedral is a grand church, an awe-inspiring place, really, and it was made more so by the fact that my daughter Rosie sang the "Ave Maria". She has a fine voice, and it sounded like an angel singing in the choir that day.

We buried my mother next to Martin Lancaster, her second husband, in his family plot in the historic Laurel Hill cemetery. I don't really know if my father or Martin were the love of her life, but Martin was faithful to her through good times and bad, and that kind of timeless love made me think that he should be the one she spends eternity with.

My mother was 98 years old when she died. It amazes me to think that she came from a place so distant in time and space from here. She was born into a land without electricity, indoor plumbing, the telephone, the automobile, the airplane or the television, and from what she told me she was hungry and barefoot for her whole childhood. Ireland wasn't a free country then, and she faced poverty and discrimination all of her young life.

She came to this country as a girl of 18, looking for something better, and she lived through enough turbulence to fill several lifetimes. I am in awe of her ability to survive, to pick herself up after each setback and get on with things. "You just put one foot in front of the other," she would always say. It was so like her, just a simple formula for how to live your life.

They were hardy people, those Irish who came over in her generation. Her friend Mary Driscoll passed away a week after my mother, and she was also 98.

I am glad my mother lived long enough to see that I straightened my life out, and at least I know I didn't disappoint her at the end. The shame of what I did in the 1930s will always haunt me, but I have tried to redeem myself at least in some small way by being a decent human being.

I am 69 years old and retired from a position at a construction company. I was in bad shape for a few years after I got out of prison, as you know, and I had a hard time finding a steady job. Luckily, though, my mother's friend Mary Driscoll helped me out. Her husband owned a firm that did brickwork, and she prevailed upon him to hire me as an office manager. I spent 12 years there before retiring last Spring, and I have a modest pension to live on.

Lucy and I live in a small house in West Philadelphia now, not far from the neighborhood where I grew up. I feel like I've traveled a great distance only to come back to my starting point. Do you remember the little boy I brought in to your store for ice cream? My grandson Pete is now 15 years old, and he's been a joy to us. He likes rock n' roll music like his mother Rosie, and he has a rebellious streak in him the way she does, but at bottom he's a good boy. Rosie is still in love with singing, and she has had some local success, singing at clubs and other entertainments, but she has to supplement her income by singing advertising jingles for various agencies in town. She wakes up every day ready for a new adventure, and more often than not she finds it.

Things are going well with Lucy, thank God. It took a long time for the wounds from my infidelity to heal, and I don't fool myself that they will ever go away entirely. I think she could have forgiven all my other mistakes easier than that. However, time has helped, and prayer, and the Grace of God. I asked for her forgiveness over and over, and she finally gave it to me.

I often think the greatest blessing of my life is that I met Lucy when I was a boy and we are still together. Why she stayed with me I do not know. If not for her I don't know what would have become of me. What made me suffer most when I was in prison was not the shame or humiliation of being in that place, it was that I didn't know if I had lost Lucy's love forever. That would have been the most crushing thing of all, and thank God it did not happen. She has over time forgiven me, and it is the most wonderful gift I could ever have.

She has taught me that forgiveness is the most precious thing of all, and it is required of all of us. For years I never forgave my father for what he did, but when you showed me the letter he wrote I understood that he had never forgiven himself for what happened when he was a boy. It warped his whole life after that, and it was the reason why he made so many mistakes later on. It was why he was constantly trying to reinvent himself; he tried to run away, but he could never run away from the secret inside him.

That taught me a lesson. I realized that I had to forgive my father, and myself. I made a horrible mistake just like he did, but I had to face up to it and finally forgive myself for it. I could not try to run from it like he did. It has helped greatly that I have such a good example in the way Lucy has forgiven me.

In a strange way this has helped me to believe in God again. For many years I did not believe, and I did not go to church. I was raised Catholic, but I lost my faith at an early age. I did not think there could be a God when I had such anger inside me, when I felt so lost and forsaken since my childhood. I did not think a God could create a world with such pain in it. All of the suffering I had seen, in my family and in the wars and economic hard times of this century, convinced me there could not be a God in charge of things.

But what I have learned is that there is such a thing as forgiveness, and that even though I don't deserve it for what I did, God poured it out on me. I received healing from Him, and so I could bestow that same healing and forgiveness on myself. And on my father. Forgiveness raises us up, makes us more than just animals who carry bitterness and revenge in our hearts.

These days Lucy and I try to stay active, and we support various causes. I have been doing what I can to support the Civil Rights movement. All men deserve to be free, to get the same chance my mother got when she came to this country. There are so many injustices, and they are caused by the dark places in the human heart. We need change desperately, and I am encouraged by the youth and energy of John F. Kennedy, our first Catholic president, and the fact that our Pope John has called for the first Vatican council in centuries to "open the window and let some air in". I think there are great things about to happen. Maybe the fires of hatred will finally be extinguished.

So you see I have tried to live a good life in the years that remained to me after I got out of prison. I made some bad mistakes, like my father, but at least I did not try to run away from them. The last time I saw my mother before she died, she told me she was proud of me. I will treasure those words till I go to my grave.

And how are you, Edith? I know my mother kept in touch with you; she was a great letter writer, and I have found replies from you in her papers. It seems as though you have made a good life for yourself in Israel, and I am happy for you. Your husband Simon is doing well, I hope. It must be a great joy for you both to be surrounded by his family, all the nieces and nephews and so on down to the next generation.

How is your daughter Mercy? I know that one of your letters said that she had finally settled down to a married life, and that she had some children. Is she still living in New Jersey? I wonder if you get to visit her very often. If you do come back, please let me know and perhaps we can meet. I would love to see you again.

We have come a long way, haven't we? It's funny how our lives are intertwined, all because of that big Irishman with the fine singing voice who came over here so many years ago. Maybe some day we'll all meet him again in Heaven and we can tell him that things worked out, that in spite of his mistakes and bad behavior we all made the best of our lives. Then again, maybe he and Rose are looking down on us now, fascinated to see what's happened in our lives, and excited to see what's going to happen next.

God's Blessing, Edith

Paul Morley

THE END OF BOOK THREE

This is the third of seven books in the Rose Of Skibbereen series. Look for the other books on Amazon at amazon.com/author/johnmcdonnell.

A word from John McDonnell:

I have been a writer all my life, but after many years of doing other types of writing I'm finally returning to my first love, which is fiction. I write in the horror, sci-fi, romance, humor and fantasy genres, and I have published 24 books on Amazon. I also write plays, and I have a YouTube channel where I post some of them. I live near Philadelphia, Pennsylvania with my wife and four children, and I am a happy man.

My books on Amazon: amazon.com/author/johnmcdonnell.

My YouTube channel:

https://www.youtube.com/user/McDonnellWrite/videos?view_as=subscriber

Look me up on Facebook at: https://www.facebook.com/JohnMcDonnellsWriting/.

Did you like this book? Did you enjoy the characters? Do you have any advice you'd like to give me? I love getting feedback on my books. Send me an email at mcdonnellwrite@gmail.com.

Find Books 1 and 2 of "Rose Of Skibbereen" here:

amazon.com/author/johnmcdonnell.

Printed in Great Britain
by Amazon